I0619273

Between My Legs

Copyright 2011 by Junnita Jackson ©

All rights reserved. No part of this book may be reproduced or transmitted in any form or by other means, electronic or mechanical, including photocopying, recording, or by any information storage and retrieval system without the express written permission from the author, except for the inclusion of brief quotes for review.

This is a work of fiction. Any resemblance to actual events or person(s) living or dead is strictly coincidental. All characters, incidents and dialog are the product of the author imagination and are in no way tied to real events or people.

Cover Design and Layout: We Read Literary Services
Published by: Verb Publishing, LLC
ISBN: 978-0578036557
LCCN: 2009935240

Printed in USA

For You,
From Me.

Dear Readers,

This is the story of my life. Candid. True. My words, not Junnita's, in case any of you have read If It Don't Hurt... It Ain't Love. You will see she has made me out to be a selfish whore. I was very unhappy with the image portrayed; so she has agreed to write my words as I have laid them out here for you.

Real Shit Always,
                    Kat

Prologue

Flowers navel level
Breathe.
Church organ playing.
Breathe.
Vaseline on teeth for bright smile.
Breathe.
Doors open.
Breathe.
Doves released.
Breathe.
Friends and family stand.
Smile.

Right foot first as I began my slow and steady walk toward Dante. He stood at the end of the aisle with Pastor Terry with a slight smile on his face. I made eye contact with him and smiled a wide smile that would force a twinkle in my eyes. But looking at Dante left my soul a little uneasy; his smile was more sinister than sincere. I shook off that thought and figured maybe it was just his nerves, being the first day of the rest of his life and all. I continued my walk slowly leaving plenty of time for photo bulbs to flash and to hear the "ooos" and "aahs" as my back revealed a very low cut silver fox fur trimmed design. I smiled at my family on my mother's side and at Dante's mother as I passed them. I finally took my place beside Dante. I passed my bouquet of calla lilies off to my maid of honor Vatyra. I smiled at each one of my bridesmaids. They all looked beautiful in the apple red dresses I picked for them. Sometime during the start of the ceremony Vatyra lit a candle for Tamia and said a quick pray for her recovery. I looked over at the groomsmen and admired Kevin in his black tux with his apple red vest and tie. I smiled at him and instead of smiling back he dropped his head. I moved on to the next groomsman and almost lost my breath. I had no idea Paul was a friend of Dante's. I remember meeting him on the train last summer and spending the evening with him. Maybe it's just a coincidence. No need to panic.

Pastor Terry began with the importance and sanctity of marriage and how precious it is in God's sight. I stifled a laugh. We prayed. Dante held my hand and squeezed. Hard. I looked up at him while every other head was bowed and he narrowed his eyes at me. He looked over his shoulder at the groomsmen. My eyes followed. My heart sank. The two guys that were in my closet a few months ago stood behind him fully clothed in wedding wear. And next to him was Steven. I hadn't seen him since the other night when I had to get him out of my apartment in a hurry. The doorman called and said Dante was on his way upstairs. He never did make it up. Why were they here?

"Amen" said the Pastor.

"Amen" said the Congregation

"Amen" said Dante' still holding his gaze on me.

My Amen was caught in my throat.

I looked at Vatyra. "What's wrong" she mouthed. I didn't answer. I just turned and stared at Dante and wondered if my silent humiliation would be enough for him. I don't think I have seen him look at anyone with so much disdain. So much... hate. I couldn't even look at him too long. I felt so guilty... no that wasn't it. I was caught out there but I wasn't sure what I felt.

"Well?" Dante asked, squeezing my hand between his. The smiled plastered on his face could have fooled anyone into thinking he was the happiest man alive right now. But I knew different looking into his eyes.

● ● ●

3

"Well what?" I asked quietly. I could feel my palms sweating in his hands. My fingers ached, he had yet to let up on the grip he had on my hand.

"Pastor Terry asked if you would have me as your husband." He said still smiling and killing me over and over with his eyes. He still wanted to marry me? Maybe there really was power in the pussy. He would be mad for a while but I guess he would get over it eventually. I would have to probably lay low..."Kat?"

"Oh... I'm sorry. Yes, of course I take you to be my husband. I do." I said in my best I-swear-I'll-be-a-good-girl-from-now-on voice. The pastor smiled and turned to Dante and asked if he also took me to be his wife forsaking all others.

"No."

What the fuck did he say?

"Excuse me?" The pastor asked. Dante cleared his throat and repeated himself.

"I said no."

I said nothing. The pastor asked if there was a reason why. Dante stepped aside giving a full view of his groomsmen.

"These men here-" he said waving his hand in their direction. "-are my lovely fiancé's..." he paused and looked at me. "you look absolutely stunning by the way." he said before continuing to address the pastor. "lovers."

"Excuse me?" The pastor asked again, not quite sure he heard right. The congregation was buzzing with questions amongst themselves. Everyone was talking at once but no one wanted to be too loud so as not to miss anything.

"Not me." Kevin said stepping out of line. Looking at Vatyra he said, "Babe I never touched her. I swear."

"Kat?" I heard Vatyra call my name. "Honey, are you all right?" I looked at Vatyra and then at the congregation. There were looks of concern and of utter disbelief. I could hear Dante address everyone explaining that he was in love with a whore. But he didn't know I was a whore when he asked to marry me, and that when he found out it was too late to cancel the wedding. I looked for a way out. I was humiliated and sick to my stomach. I could feel the back of my neck start to sweat, and the sensation that all eyes were on me were overwhelming.

The hell with them.

The hell with Dante'.

I looked at him and then at the rock on my finger. My engagement ring, six carat cushion cut solitaire. Most people come down the aisle with a naked ring finger on their wedding day. I was having no parts of that; I wanted my ring very visible in my pre-wedding photos. I considered causing a bigger scene which included me throwing the ring at him and calling him a liar, but that was a fleeting thought. I decided to hightail it on out of there before I was bombarded with a ton of questions I had no answers to. So much for the power of the pussy.

Chapter One

Fuck Dante. I didn't need him anyway. How dare he put my private life on blast? This is straight bull shit. I ran down the aisle of the church, briefly making eye contact with Vatyra's mother. I pushed my way through the double doors and almost stopped to admire the sparkling lights. The ballroom was decked out in bright twinkling lights; hundreds of shimmering helium balloons were floated up to the ceilings. Attached to each balloon was a string of lights that fell to about five feet above the ground, some even came lower maybe two or three feet off the ground. The tables were draped in white silk linens, each topped with an amazing centerpiece of calla lilies and baby's breath in beautiful crystal vases and at the bottom of each vase swam a bright red tropical fish.

I remembered telling the florist I didn't care what type of fish it was as long as it was red and you couldn't get it in your local pet store. I stopped, briefly, when I saw the ice sculpture on the cake table. Dante took care of that. That was the first time I saw it. It was a huge picture frame; made entirely of ice. It looked a lot like those heavy crystal wedding frames people give as gifts. It had our initials carved into it. There was a picture of us at a picnic laying on the grass kissing. I remember the picture and the day. I was studying the picture, thinking about how the couple in it looks so damn in love. For a moment I wondered what was real; was it what I saw in the picture or was it...

Vatyra's calls snapped me out of my trance and I continued my way out the side doors to where the horse and carriages were waiting. I ordered ten to take the guest on a carriage ride around the estate. Each was stocked with a fox fur blanket to protect against the cold and a bottle of champagne. All the horses were all white including the tails. I went to the one decorated with white ribbons and got in. I pulled my dress around me until the hem of the back of my dress laid in my lap.

"Go!" I yelled at the driver. The driver began toward the trail around the estate. "No go anywhere but here!"

"Where ma'am?" The driver questioned his accent Caribbean thick. I tingled. I had to smile to myself; I'm already shit out of luck and playing runaway bride, but just that fast his voice made me want to hide him under the skirt of my dress. "Ma'am?"

I looked around and exhale.

"Please just go." I said quietly. I closed my eyes as I felt the horses pull the carriage forward. The air was crisp. I noticed the blanket on the seat beside me and pulled it around me. Under the blanket was a satin bridal bag, I picked it up and ran my fingers over the beading. Vatyra picked this bag out months ago. She must have put it in here. I opened the bag and pulled out a sealed envelope, two passports and 2 envelopes with airline tickets. I quickly opened the passports there was one for me and one for Dante. Same for the airline tickets, one for me and one for him. I opened the envelope and saw a congratulations card with five crisp hundred dollar bills and $5000 worth of Travelers Cheques. I almost forgot about the cheques Vatyra convinced me to get them when we were having lunch one day.

"What if you lose your wallet while in Barbados?" She questioned.

"Your life is full of what ifs, isn't it?" I countered as I slid my American Express to the bank teller for checks.

I could kiss her paranoid ass right now. "Take me to the airport." I ordered. I looked at the airline tickets again and remembered we weren't supposed to leave until tomorrow afternoon. Maybe I should go home and get my bags; I looked back in the bag and saw nothing else. No keys. I could always have the doorman let me into my apartment. But I didn't want to have to explain myself. Fuck that why should I have to explain myself, my rent pays his salary. I started to wonder what was worse, having to explain or having people speculate about what happened.

"De airport, ma'am?" The Sweet Caribbean Voice questioned.

"That's what I said."

"De airport es 'bout seven miles away, dis ole gal," he said nodding toward the horse, "she only does 'bout five miles en hour. So we are talking about a good hour ant a haf befo' we get dere. Not ta mention I'm not sure it tis legal ta have de horse and carriage on de highway."

"Okay, okay. Take me to the nearest mall. So I can get a change of clothes then I can call a cab from there."

"Tis Sunday."

"So?" I sighed heavily. The carriage had settled into a motion of back and forth sways. The air was crisp and I could feel my nose starting to run. I pulled the blanket up further and snuggled into it. I peered out into the night and wondered what the fuck. What the Fuck! WHAT THE FUCK! I wanted to scream. The hoofs made a steady clip-clop sound on the pavement. The sky was lit up by the moon. I wanted to cry but I was not going to give Dante the satisfaction.

"So, de mall tis close'. Tis afta seven in de evening." Sweet Caribbean Voice said, and then added. "Ere ting ire?"

"Sure." I answered. "Just peaches and roses."

"Still wan' de airport?"

"Sure." I closed my eyes and couldn't help but to replay Dante's words in my head.

"These men here, are my lovely fiance's... you look absolutely stunning by the way... lovers."

"Power of the pussy-" I mumbled to myself, not believing I fooled even myself with that shit. Fuck him! My head was pounding and I swore I heard sirens. I want to go the airport. I want to get away from this hell hole.

"Ma'am?"

"What? Oh···um, nothing. Do you have a cell phone?"

"No" Sweet Caribbean voice said. "We aren't allowed ta have dem on while workin' so I left me cell back at de job."

"What do you do if you are in trouble or need help?" I asked still not being able to completely comprehend the day or my life for that either.

"Dis." he said holding up a walkie- talkie.

"Can you call me a cab with that thing?"

"'Fraid not can only call back ta de estate."

I looked beyond the driver and saw he was headed toward an IHOP. I could use the phone there. I told the driver to pull over and see if he could use their phone to call me a cab. He pulled up into the parking lot and jumped out flashing me a wide white toothed smile. I gave him a weak smile in return. I watched him disappear into the restaurant before leaning my head back and closing my eyes. The vision of Dante's eyes assaulted me behind my closed lids. The pain. The fury. I couldn't recall him ever looking at me that way. I was a stranger to him while standing at the altar.

Sweet Caribbean came out of IHOP and announced the cab would be here in about 15 minutes. I nodded okay without opening my eyes.

"Wan' me wait wit cha'?" He asked. "Ya startin' to draw a crowd."

"Yes, thank you." I answered, opening my eyes to look into his. He wore an expression of understanding, but how could that be? He didn't know me. I studied his eyes and found no pity. His look was of genuine concern, no judgments. This specimen of a man was fine. He was the color of wet cement and his body looked as if it had been chiseled out of concrete. His hair was pulled into a ponytail of dreads. Each lock looked as if it was oiled and loved individually. He smelled of mangoes and a hint of almond. I watched his lips move as he talked to me but heaven help me I ain't heard a word he said. His tongue moved to lick his lips and brought my attention to the tiny patch of hair under the center of his bottom lip. Lil Kat pulsated. I exhaled and redirected my focus to his massive hands which he now blew into to warm. Nice large hands with thick fingers and... a platinum wedding band. That explains the twinkle in his eyes.

I asked him to go to the gas station across the street and get me a bottle of water and a pack of Aleve. While he was gone I started removing the pins from my hair. All these bobby pins felt like they were each stabbing me in my brain. I swear I am being killed slowly on this day. A sound of loud laughter made me look up. A group of teenagers walked up to the IHOP door and was laughing and joking with one another. I made eye contact with one of the girls; she was brown skinned with almond shaped eyes. She looks like she couldn't be more than 16 or 17 years old. I wondered about her life; briefly wondered if she was happy. She seemed to be; she was laughing as she backed into the front door of the restaurant opening it with her ample behind. I heard her remark to her friend that my wedding dress was off the chain. Then I heard another reply "she probably got stood up. Who comes to IHOP in their wedding dress?" Then they all laughed, except for the girl with the almond eyes. Her laughter faded into a look of sorrow. I broke eye contact. I didn't need her pity. I looked around and notice several other people either sitting in their cars or standing outside of them looking in my direction. Children wanted to pet the horse and others commented on if I was going to or returning from my wedding. Camera phones were held up in my direction. This was just great. I had better not find my picture up on you-tube or somebodies Facebook page.

Sweet Caribbean Voice bounded his way across traffic towards me. I could feel my heart race as I watched his dick swing back and forth beneath his trousers. Damn he was definitely a boxer's man, no punk panties in his future. I licked my lips and wondered if I had time for a little fuck-me-therapy. Some women shoe shop, I fuck. No attachments. See what happens when you get men trying to label you. They like to use words like "wifey" and "marriage" and shit like that. Then you end up waiting for a yellow cab, trying to ignore the rumble in your belly from the smell of pancakes coming from inside of a damn IHOP, while trying to forget the fact that your friends and family are talking about you over a glorious five course meal that you picked the fuck out at damn near $200 a plate.

"Here you go." He said breaking me out of my ranting thoughts while handing me a plastic white shopping bag. He then handed me back the $100 bill I had given him.

"What happened?" I asked looking at the bill. "I'm gonna need change for the cab."

"Don' worry 'bout it. Only cost $2. I tink dey don't change anyting more den a $50." He took the bill out my hand and walked back into the IHOP; after a few minutes he returned with an IHOP takeout bag and ninety-something dollars in change. "I bought some biscuits" He said digging in his pocket and counting out some money to pay for the biscuits.

"Don't worry about it" I said. "Anyway here is my cab." A yellow cab pulled into the parking lot and parked in front of the restaurant doors. He beeped twice. I grabbed my blanket and my bridal bag and climbed out of the carriage. I walked over to the cab, pulled on the door handle and climbed in. I gathered my dress into my lap and Sweet Caribbean Voice closed the door. He tapped on the window and I rolled it down.

"Don' listen to de devils lies." He said simply before backing away from the cab.

I didn't respond.

"Where to?" The cabbie asked.

"Airport."

The cab pulled out the parking lot. I reached for the door to roll the window back up when Sweet Caribbean Voice spoke again.

"Dere es more power en prayer den pussy."

Again, I didn't respond.

Chapter Two

The cab jumped on 95 South toward the airport. I looked out the window and watched as cars zoomed past down the highway. My life, like these cars, was a blur. I looked through the bullet proof glass that separated me from the driver, out the front windshield and saw a sign that said Philadelphia Airport Exit 2 miles.

"Driver I have to make a stop before we go to the airport." I gave the cabbie my home address. I figured I should really try to change my clothes. I could even pack a quick bag.

After about twenty minutes or so the cab pulled up in front of my apartment building. I told the cab I would be right out. I ran inside and greeted the night doorman.

"Hello, Mr. Baily. I really need to get into my apartment. Can you call for maintenance to let me in?"

Mr. Baily looked at me curiously. Questions I hoped he wouldn't ask were written all over his face.

"Did the movers forget something, ma'am?" He asked, still looking at me like I was out of place.

"Movers?" I asked. Then it hit me. Dante had movers pack my stuff and take it to his house and put my furniture in storage. "Damn. Are they still up there?"

"No ma'am. They started shortly after you left this morning to prepare for your wedding. Truth be told I didn't reckon I'd be laying eyes on you again. Is there a problem?"

"No, I just need to get some things." I responded as I headed back to the cab. The cold air sent a chill across my bare shoulders and down my naked back. I gathered my skirt around me and slammed the car door once I was safely inside.

"Where to?" The driver asked.

"The airport." I answered. I looked out the window and fought back my frustration. Will nothing go my way today? I had to take a picture by an ugly tree, I got rejected at the alter and now I can't get my damn clothes, because I don't have a set of keys on me. And just about everybody I know is at the damn estate in Bala Cynwyd. The driver jumped back on 95 south and I stared out the window trying to decide what the fuck to do. My bags I packed for our honeymoon were in the room we were supposed to stay in at the estate. This is bullshit. A huge billboard for Smirnoff Vodka stared back at me as traffic slowed. Four lanes of traffic damn neared stopped. Yeah, vodka sounded good right about now. I could go for a little numb-my-soul in a bottle right about now.

The driver took the appropriate exit for the airport. A few minutes later I was shoving two twenties into the pay slot in the bullet proof glass.

"Keep the change." I said as I exited the cab. I looked up at the massive structure in front of me better known as the Philadelphia International Airport. I walked toward the huge doors and they parted to let me walk through them. I pulled my ticket and passport out of my bag and headed toward the desk with the United sign above it. There was only one person in front of me but when I stood behind her she told me to go ahead after taking in my whole appearance.

"May I help you?" The young woman at the counter asked. I stepped to the counter and laid my passport and the two airline tickets in front of her.

"Yes, when is the next flight to Barbados?" I questioned. The young woman with the fire red hair and the heavy southern drawl tapped a couple of keys on her keyboard and told me there is a flight leaving at 10:20 pm with a connecting flight in NYC.

"These tickets are for tomorrow afternoon and I would like to change the flight for this ticket and I would like to cancel this ticket all together." I said pointing out my ticket to change and Dante's ticket to cancel. "You should have my credit card information on file."

"Okay, the flight for this evening will be $2453.67..."

"What? I didn't pay that much for the two tickets together." I protested.

"The only seat we have available is in First class. Plus there is a fee for canceling less than 24 hours prior to the flight. Did you want me to continue processing your ticket?' She asked in that I'm-so-damn-helpful voice.

"Whateva." I sighed and whipped out the travelers checks to pay the difference of the tickets.

"Okay, I'm gonna need the credit card you booked the flight with and some ID." She said.

I exhaled and sucked my teeth.

"Look at me." I said between clenched teeth. "Have you not noticed me standing here in a wedding dress?"

"Yes, I did. However, our policy dictates what is required to purchase airline tickets."

She said in a don't-make-me-show-you-who-I-really-am-outside-of-here voice.

"Is there a problem?" A woman dressed in a business suit asked.

"Yes, she needs to make some changes on her ticket but is lacking the proper items to complete the transaction."

"I will handle it, Vickie. Please take the next person in line. Miss, can you step over here please?"

I told the woman what I needed, she pushed a few buttons on her little keyboard and a couple of beeps later she printed out a credit slip for Dante's ticket and gave me a new ticket for a flight leaving in about an hour and forty-five minutes. She explained they didn't keep credit cards on file and she couldn't credit the ticket back to my card but I could purchase future tickets with the credit slip as long as I didn't lose it. She sighed at me and asked was there anything else she could do. I asked if there were any boutiques open that I could get a change of clothes. She looked at her watch and then toward the security checkpoints and told me I would never make it. She apologized and walked away.

I moved steadily through airport security while watching people watch me. After a while a woman in a security uniform carrying a walkie-talkie asked me to step out of line and follow her.

"Is there a problem miss?" I asked as I passed through the rope barrier she held open for me.

She didn't respond.

"Excuse me." I said stopping. "Is there a problem?" I asked again. "I have dealt with just about all the shit I can handle tonight."

The security guard stopped and turned around to face me. She pointed beyond me towards the front of the security check point. I turned in the direction she was pointing and saw people against walls and on benches slowly putting on their shoes and retrieving their belongings from the huge plastic tubs that went through the X-ray machine. They were all glancing in my direction and then back to what they were doing. They were trying to hide the fact they were watching me.

"Who do you think they are waiting for?" She asked as she turned around and continued toward a door marked Security. She produced a key from her waist on a stretchy cord and opened the door. I followed her in. Another female security guard was sitting in a chair against a wall. The first guard picked up her metal wand and told me to raise my arms. I did as I was told fighting back the sudden urge to scream and cry. She waved the wand over my chest and down the front of my dress and it came to life.

What now. I thought.

"I'm sorry; we are going to have to ask you to remove your top." The 1st guard said, sighing.

"Is your dress boned?" The 2nd guard asked.

"Yes." I said. "The boning is made of steel."

"We are going to have to remove it. Do you have something you could put on?"

"No, I don't." I said still fighting my emotions as they rushed to explode from me.

"Okay, maybe we can just flip this down and pull the boning out without you having to get undressed." She said, bending the top of my dress down at the waist. I put my forearm over my breast to hide my nipples. What was I thinking not wearing any underwear? She took a small pocket knife out and made little slits in the fabric above the small strips of metal. I wanted to cry. With a small pair of tweezers she gently tugged at each of the metal strips. Each tug left me feeling more humiliated then the tug before. Twenty five strips in all. I fastened my gown as I looked at the small pile of metal being secured in a plastic zip lock bag. I watched, while I redressed, as the 1st guard wrote the date and time with a sharpie.

"Since the edges of these are rounded we will let you go on and catch your flight; if they were sharp we would have had to detain you. You are free to go." She said passing the wand over my body once more for good measure.

I looked at the clock on the wall and noticed I barely had 20 minutes to get to my gate. I released a frustrated moan, picked up my bridal bag (which they also scanned) and headed out the door. There was a small crowd mulling around the security office, some of the same faces I'd glimpsed before going in.

"Don't you people have a plane to catch?" I yelled and watched the crowd thin out with the help of other security guards.

I followed the signs to my gate and was surprised I was actually pretty close. I checked the digital board which stated they would be boarding my flight in less than 5 minutes. I ignored all the pointing and stares and stepped into a small book store. I looked on the shelves and bought a copy of ESSENCE and Time Magazine with Obama on the cover. I also bought a journal and a pen. My Journal was packed away with my stuff, possibly sitting on the floor in a box at Dante's house. I'll just have to start a new one. I exited the store just in time to hear the attendants say they were boarding first class seats. I could feel the curious looks boring a hole into me, but I refused to make eye contact. I held my head high, gave the attendant my ticket and proceeded down the walkway to board the plane.

* * *

Chapter Three

I looked down at the blank pages of my journal and sighed. The pages may have been empty but my mind was bursting. I put pen to paper and began.

Dear Journal,

I stopped. There wasn't anything my journal hadn't already held secret for me. I wasn't ready to relive this day yet. I closed the journal and leaned my head back against the head rest. I stared at the little reading lights above me until my eyes grew dry from not blinking. I closed them and exhaled. The gentleman next to me shifted in his seat. I opened my eyes and turned to my left. He looked at me and then at my wedding dress, which was once a beautiful sight to behold, now it was nothing more than a reminder of a day gone horribly wrong.

"Interesting day?" He asked. I briefly wondered if he was baiting me for conversation. He was young; maybe early twenties. He wore a dark blue sweater and a pair of equally dark jeans. The colors made his grey eyes sparkle and his walnut skin complimented his eyes well. He could have done without the baseball cap though.

"You don't know the half and I ain't in the mood." I casually responded. I turned to my right to stare out of the window. The sky was burnt as we ascended upwards. This used to be my favorite part of flying, the takeoff. I use to close my eyes and pretend this was my rise to a luxurious life, leaving all things undesirable on the ground. Flying always made me feel like anything in life was possible. Now even flying is tainted with that whole debacle of a wedding.

How the fuck did I get here? I thought. My mind wandered back to him. Not Dante' but him. Mr. Heart Breaker. I opened my journal again.

Time heals all wounds. What a crock of shit! I have been walking around carrying this gaping hole in my heart for more than 14 years, Journal. It's not fair. I can't shake him. He...is...in...me. My soul is still infected with him. The scent of him still lingers in my nose. It doesn't help that I bought Dante the same cologne he wears just so I can keep the scent

of him near me. His touch still lingers on the base of
my spine. My all I gave to him. I still remember it
all...

I turned to look at the man next to me to see if he was trying to read my journal. He wasn't. The stewardess was coming down the aisle with her drink cart. She stopped and asked if I needed anything. I told her I wanted a shot of something hard and I didn't care what it was. She gave me a shot bottle of vodka and a small plastic cup with some ice. I took the top off the bottle and drank. Two swallows later it was gone. I put the cup on the tray from the seat in front of me. I reread the last line I wrote.

I still remember it all...

I closed my eyes as my breath caught in my throat. No more tears for him. This is bullshit. I exhaled and remembered those journal entries from years ago⋯

Dear Journal,
The rabbit died, just as simple as that. I remembered
my mother telling me that was how she told my
father she was pregnant with me. I keep staring at
those pregnancy tests; I kept wishing the plus will
turn to minus, the pink line blue and the double lines
to single. But they ain't changing. I was hoping to

wait until school was done to have a family with him, but I don't have that many classes left. I could do both. Journal my excitement is growing. What will he say? Will he want a boy or girl? What is that thing people always say…oh yes "I don't care as long as it's healthy." Why can't they wish for healthy and the sex of their choice? Doesn't make sense. I stood for about an hour in the mirror, just staring. I puffed my belly out and caressed its roundness.

He'll be here soon. I'm wondering how to tell him. Should I just show him the test and let him come to his conclusions on his own. Maybe a time will just present itself at dinner tonight. I think that's him honking now. Wish me luck.

Until Later

Dear Journal,

Dinner was Wonderful. I told him I was pregnant as soon as we were seated at our table. I couldn't help it. I couldn't hold it in. I just blurted it out. I'm convinced I sounded like a damn idiot. He asked me what kind of wine I wanted to drink and I said no wine for me because I'm having your baby. Oh Shit. I can't believe I said it like that. But Journal, he grabbed my hand and looked into my eyes and told me he loved me. He loves me. He always implied it before but this time he actually said it. I don't remember much else besides rambling off possible baby names and having to look for a baby doctor to care for me during my pregnancy. He just looked at me and listened. He was so understanding about my concerns of school. I just know he is happy for us. He didn't mention marriage but I know it's coming, he's not the kind of guy that would let his kid grow up with no father. Mr. and Mrs. Oh snap! This is so unbelievable. I am on top of the world. He said he wanted to take me somewhere tomorrow. I can't wait. Maybe it's ring shopping.

Until later.

Dear journal,
It's been three days, but I haven't written because I still can't believe it went down the way it did. Such BULLSHIT. I can't even find the words. So, last I told you he was supposed to be taking me someplace, someplace special I thought or maybe even ring shopping to celebrate our upcoming nuptials. Journal I'm such an idiot. I should have known better when I saw all the angry faces carrying signs that read "It's a life" "Abortion is murder" and the ultimate didn't have any words at all just a picture of a bloody deformed fetus stuck in a large jar with some kind of suction device attached

to it. My mind didn't even register that this was the horrible place he was taking me too. I was still sitting in the passenger side of his car grinning and thinking about my damn ring. I remember thinking about how bad I felt for people whose circumstances led them to these clinics. And here I am looking at him all confused as he parked and opened the passenger door to help me out.

And after the confusion, came the humiliation as I climbed out of the car, smile fading from my face as the realization dawned on me. The long walk from the car to the front door of the clinic broke something in me. The picketers were aggressive with yelling phrases of hatred for people who aborted their child. But wasn't it a woman's choice, what she did with her body? But this··· shit··· was not my choice. Someone spit in my face and pointed to the wordless sign showing the jarred baby. I grabbed my stomach. I tried to protect it from the negativity. I looked at him and none of it seemed to faze him. That turned my stomach worse than the second glob of spit that landed on my chin. I froze and turned toward the car. I could go back, I should go back. This baby belonged to me even if he wouldn't claim it. But he told me he loved me. I turned to him and I said

"You told me you loved me."

"I do."

"So why are we here?"

"I don't want any more children."

"Anymore?"

"Yes, I have three children. All are about your age. Plus it wouldn't be fair to my wife."

"Your wife?"

"Yes, Katherine. I'm married."

"No I've stayed at your place. We've dated for over a year. What the hell are you talking about?"

"That is a little place I keep near campus. Let's go."

He grabbed my elbow and led me toward the door. The picketers were harassing someone else now. He announced our appointment to the receptionist and handed me the clipboard she gave him. I refused to take it. I told him he could stick that clipboard up his ass. He began filling out the information the best he knew how. He got most of it right. I knocked the clipboard to the floor when he filled out RELATIONSHIP TO PATIENT as DAUGHTER. The nurse called my name and took me in the back. While I was walking back there I yelled…

"I'm not his fucking daughter. I'm half his age. He knocked me up and he lied to me about being married. He's my fucking college professor. His name is David Paul Besten and he teaches at Temple

• • •

University. Lock up your daughters. Who can you trust? Not your elders, not your teachers···"

The nurse asked if I was alright. I told her to get this fucking baby out of me now. More than an hour later I walked past David sitting in the waiting room as I headed out to the parking lot and got into the back seat of Tamia's bucket and cried into Tamia's lap while Vatyra drove us to her mom's house. The nurse told me I needed a ride home and did I need to call anyone so I had her call them and explain the situation. They didn't ask me about it either, they just let me grieve··· Fuck him. Fuck Men!

Until later

Dear Journal,

My heart is aching. The light in my soul is being depleted. As my soul darkens, my desire to hate him is in a battle with my soul's need to love him. I long for the days when he belonged just to me. No ghosts of wives or girlfriends. I found myself following him until the day I saw him with her; then I began following her. I followed her everywhere, to the grocery store, hair salon and lunch with her girlfriends. Journal, my need to strike her with my car or fuck her up with a bag of nickels is strong. I've never really been a violent person but I want someone to hurt as much as I do right now. The thought of his lips on hers makes me ill, and the audacity of him to take me as his mistress.

My educated mind cannot comprehend his deceit. Why lie to me? The more I think about it the more my intelligence is insulted. Deceit by omission still makes him a liar and a cheat. My rational mind says that's enough to walk away. But is it?

Help me, Journal. I've never thought of myself as one of THOSE women. Did I confuse sex with love? I'm pretty sure I did not. The sex was great but it wasn't forget-who-the-hell-you-are-and-lose-your-dignity great. It was more like weak-knees-bruised-thighs great. Maybe I-want-to-tell-my-girls-but-don't-want-them-fantasizing-about-my-man great, but definitely not amnesia chick great. This was bullshit. Maybe just···maybe I could walk away without this getting ugly. But hell, he gave me every indication I was the love of his life. Flowers, Jewels, Expensive dinners. He even hooked me up with my own apartment fully furnished. What college girl has that?

OH SHIT? Journal, I do believe I was being kept···

Until Later

I exhaled again and wiped away my tears.

• • •

Chapter Four

I unbuckled my seat belt as the captain announced we safely touched ground. I wasn't in the mood for this shit. I had already drunk 3 bottles of the damn tiny wine and was ready to explode at the first person who looked at me funny. I didn't have any luggage in the overhead compartment so I stood, gathered my dress around me and pushed past the people in the isle without so much as a "get out of my fucking way". I headed for the front of the plane just to be stopped by the stewardess.

"Will you be needing any assistance?" Her look of pity ignited the fuse I was barely trying to contain.

"Do I look like I need any fucking assistance?" I countered my voice barely above a whisper. I turned to face the crowd that gathered in the isle behind me, waiting patiently to exit the plane. "What? Has none of you ever seen a bride on her wedding day?"

"I just thought that maybe you needed someone to talk to. I'm off and I don't have any immediate plans. I also thought you might need a change of clothes and we are about the same size." She said quietly.

I thought for a minute before responding.

"I don't need your charity." I sighed deeply and walked off the plane. I walked down that long hall connecting the plane to the airport and thought about how I must look to the average Joe. I needed to change my clothes bad. I glanced over my shoulder as I clutched my bridal bag with my journals and magazines in it to my chest. I suddenly felt ⋯ embarrassed to be walking around the airport in my not so white wedding dress. I took a deep breath and pushed forward. I wasn't sure of the time but the sun was barely down here. Maybe the shops were still open and I could find an outfit. I walked past the desk and the rope that held back the people not exiting the plane. I was looking down past the rows of chairs in the waiting area and trying to see which way was the gift shops when a bright light blinded me.

"Excuse me miss, what's your name?" One voice asked.

"Why are you traveling in your wedding dress, miss?" Yet another asked.

"Left at the altar? Tell us about it. Channel 4. Give us an exclusive." Someone else shouted.

What the fuck?! Fucking reporters? You have got to be kidding me. I tried to back up through the doors toward the plane but the crowd continued to push me forward as the flash bulbs continued to pop.

"This way." A familiar voice said as I felt my arm being pulled in a direction away from the commotion. I could feel the tears welling up in my eyes. Damn, all this because I like to fuck.

"Thank you." I stated as I tried not to look directly at the stewardess. She rolled her luggage into the ladies room and closed the door behind her. I watched her as she leaned her back against the door. "What is with the reporters?"

"I'm not sure; I think some rapper is here?" She said looking at me slowly from head to toe. "Would you like a change of clothes? I've some jeans and a tee shirt that would fit you. If you go back out there like that... well you would be walking into another media frenzy."

I looked down at my dress and just nodded. "I'm a size 8."

"I'm a six, so my jeans may not fit··· but," she said as she unzipped her luggage and pulled out a pair of black Baby Phat sweats. "These might fit.

They are a medium. Just tighten the drawstring if they are too big."

"Thanks." I said wondering what the hell I got myself into. I could still hear the reporters outside the door. I didn't want her to know I didn't have on any underwear so I pulled up the skirt of my dress and stepped into the sweatpants one leg at a time. I pulled them up over my hips and pulled the drawstrings tight.

"Here, turn around. Let me unzip you." She said turning me slowly by my shoulders. "This dress is stunning."

"This dress is trash." I sighed and stepped out of it after it was unzipped. I bent to pick it up with one hand and used my other hand and forearm to cover my naked breast. I grabbed a handful of the heap of wedding dress and dragged it to the trash can in the corner.

"No. You can't throw that away."

"Yes. I can and I am. I appreciate your help···um···"

"Nicole."

"Sorry, Nicole, I just don't need it or want it anymore for that matter." I briefly thought about all those pictures I paid a nice penny for and will never see. The photographer I hired for the wedding was expensive, but he came highly recommended, even if he did want me to take a picture by that ugly tree.

I held my hand out to accept the T-Shirt she was handing me. It was a purple baby tee with the words "SHIT HAPPENS" imprinted on it.

"Appropriate." I chuckled as I slid the shirt over my head. I looked down at myself and wiggled my toes. "You wouldn't happen to have an extra pair of shoes in there would you?"

"Where are your shoes?" She asked, noticing my bare feet for the first time.

I held up my bulging bridal bag. I took one shoe out and tossed it in the trash and then the other.

"4 inch satin pumps don't exactly go with sweats." I stood quiet while she searched her bag and pulled out a plastic drawstring bag with the word AVON printed on it.

"These are flip flops; brand new. You can have them. Sorry that's all I have, I know it's cold out…"

"Don't worry about it." I said taking the flip flops. "Where I'm headed will be plenty warm."

"I want those shoes." She said fetching them from the trash. She peered into the inside of the shoe and found the size. "Just my size." She said in a sing song voice as she tossed them into her bag. She looked me up and down before she decided to give me the sweat jacket that matched the pants.

• • •

"Thank you." I said again. I threw the flip flops to the ground one at a time and slid my recently pedicured feet into them. "This has been a long day. I'm sorry I was nasty to you earlier."

"Coffee?" She asked.

"I could use a cup." I put the hood from my jacket on my head and opened the door to exit the bathroom.

A flash bulb popped in my face.

"That's not her. Sorry miss." Someone said

"Did you see the woman in the wedding dress?" Another asked.

"She is still in there crying. Give her a minute, you vultures'." Nicole hissed at the reporters. "Don't you have anything better to do than to report on people's private lives?"

I walked in front of Nicole toward a small coffee shop near a gift shop selling silk scarves. I took a seat at a small table in the corner and watched as Nicole pulled her suitcase behind her toward the counter. I heard her order 2 large coffees with cream and sugar on the side and 2 large cranberry muffins.

She came and sat at the table and set the items down. The sight of the muffins made me remember just how hungry I was. I thanked her and immediately began eating the muffin giving the coffee time to cool off. I could see the steam coming out of the top of the cup. I turned my head to look in the direction we just came from. The bathroom door had a nice crowd in front of it and airport security was now running down the hall to see what the commotion was all about. I heard a reporter state no one was in the bathroom. I glanced at Nicole as we both smiled at the man with the camera holding up a wedding dress we know he pulled from the trash. What a fucking waste.

"What's your name?" Nicole asked, breaking into my thoughts.

"You can call me Kat." I said plainly.

"Ok Kat. Feel like talking?"

"No."

"Hum··· Okay." Nicole looked at her watch and started to stand. "Well at any rate, I'm glad to have been of some assistance to you. Good luck and thanks for the shoes."

"I refused to love him."

Nicole sat back down cautiously, looking at me with one eyebrow raised. She waited for me to continue.

"He didn't deserve how I treated him. He didn't need to feel the pain I saw in his eyes. I didn't want to feel anything for Dante at all. I fought it. Every time I thought I was falling in love with him. I went out and fucked someone; his friends, his family, strangers. It didn't matter as long as I could get Dante off my heart for a little while. I never thought he was gonna find out."

"Did you love him?"

"I think a better question is did I love me?"

"Did you love you?"

"I don't even know me."

"That's deep."

"That's sad."

"How did he find out?"

"I don't know. Hell, I even slept with his assistant."

"How do you even know he knew? "

I laughed.

I sighed.

And then I cried.

I mean I really cried.

I looked at Nicole, sitting there patiently waiting, waiting for an answer. I couldn't help but wonder what makes her tick. She don't know me. Why help me. I stared deep into her large brown eyes and thought this plain Jane was sincerely concerned. I felt no malicious intent or shadiness coming from her. She was just being who she was. She made it seem so simple. It made me wonder even more what kind of person I really was. I pushed the thought from my mind that was too deep to focus on right now.

• • •

"Why do you care?" I asked while I tried not to sound ungrateful in my question. I was just curious.

"I don't. You look like you needed something. You look lost. My mom, rest her soul, she used to say it helps to talk and it doesn't hurt to listen. I got nothing else to do until the connecting flight to Barbados gets here." She pinched a cranberry out her muffin and popped it into her mouth.

"I'm on that flight too. I think." I unzipped the jacket I was wearing and pulled the bridal bag out of the waistband and took out my connecting flight ticket and handed it to her. She confirmed it was the same flight and I put the ticket away.

"How do you know he knew?" She repeated.

"Because he told me so."

"So, if you knew he knew what's with the runaway bride thing?"

"He told me⋯" I cleared my throat while avoiding eye contact. "at the wedding. He told everyone at the wedding. Did I mention we were standing at the altar?" I decided to leave out the part about the groomsman. I wasn't even sure that part really happened.

"Wow, talk about your Lifetime special. I can see why you are upset and running through the airport in your wedding dress." She took the lid off her coffee and blew in it after dropping some creamer in it. "You're stronger than I am. Girl, I would be held up in a corner somewhere crying my eyes out."

"I just wanted to get out of there. He totally embarrassed me; one minute I was saying 'I do' and the next minute he was saying 'I don't' and calling me a whore, in front of the entire congregation."

"Damn. I'm sorry. Now what?"

"Barbados." I said while stuffing the last bit of cranberry muffin into my mouth. We sat in silence for a while before I said. "I think I loved him."

"Oh?"'

"Oh⋯ What?"

"You said you think you love him. Why were you getting married if you weren't sure you loved him?"

"I'm thirty-something years old." I said matter-of- factly.

"So?" She asked, before getting up to request a cup of ice from the counter. I thought about her very simple question as I watched her take the lid off her coffee again and scoop some ice onto a spoon and put it into her coffee before returning the lid. "That should cool it down quicker." She said to herself and then repeated her question to me.

"So⋯" I said thinking of an honest answer and not the bullshit I usually give to everyone else. "So I fucked up. I loved him; but I didn't want to. Too much work, too many compromises. And honestly I don't want to be responsible for how I make other people feel. I'm not trying to be the reason someone is happy, because the flip side of that coin is I will also eventually be the reason that person is unhappy."

"Selfish?"

"Very." She smiled at my answer and then asked if I was selfish or just scared. I told her maybe a bit of both. We sat and talked a little more about this and that before she asked what I was going to be doing in Barbados.

"I don't know. Might just relax, do a little shopping and a bit of self-reflection." She gave me her cell number and told me to call if I needed anything while in Barbados that she would be there for a few weeks visiting family. I told her I would while she gathered her stuff and she had to go check in with the pilots. "Okay see you on the plane. And thanks again for the clothes."

I looked at the paper she gave me with her number on it and balled it up in my muffin wrapper before throwing it in the trash.

I got enough friends.

Chapter Five

Arriving in Barbados, I stepped off the plane and deeply inhaled, filling my lungs with a second chance. This shit was so crazy, could I really just pick up and start over outside the country with just about nothing to my name but a few travelers checks? I guess I would find out soon enough. I walked through the airport and caught local transportation to my hotel. After settling into an absolutely gorgeous room with a view of the white sand beach I decided to take a walk and see what I could see. Truth be told I was restless and needed a change of clothes. So off I go in search of the local shopping area. After a few minutes of walking I spotted a display of postcards and thought of the people I left behind. They were probably worried. I walked over to the display and looked at each postcard. I chose three. Each said Barbados but they all had different scenarios. There was a beautiful sunset with shades of purple and orange, another showed the bluest ocean I'd ever seen and the last was a basic resort pool side shot.

"How much?" I asked the old woman overseeing the display. She just scrunched up her nose like she smelled something bad, so I repeated my question. "How much?"

The old woman cocked her head to the side and spoke one word.

"Excuse me?" I asked.

"Karma." She repeated.

"What?"

She pointed her crooked finger at me and repeated herself. "Karma."

"Knock it off, you creeping me out." I said. "How much?"

"Karma···karma···karma" She chanted, her eyes never leaving me.

"What about it?" I asked, half expecting her to say 'Karma' again. I laid five US dollars on the counter and waited for her response. She snatched the money and stuck it in her bra.

No shame.

"You gon' soon find out." She stated her accent thick with Caribbean spices. I looked up at the old woman and studied her for a moment. She looked ancient with her sagged skin and dull discolored eyes. Try as I might I could not pinpoint any one shade of color; her eyes were a blend of grey, green and white. I imagined she would be toothless but couldn't confirm that at the moment. Her hair was a mangled mass of grey and white stringy curls. Looking at her the old saying 'What goes around comes around' popped into my head. I narrowed my eyes at the old woman pursed my lips and turned to leave.

"Karma." The old woman whispered.

"You don't fuckin' know me." I hissed, rolling my eyes. The old woman chuckled as if knowing an inside joke. "And give me my change, old woman, those cards were only .59 each." I pointed at a sign I hadn't noticed earlier and I held out my hand to receive my change. The old woman grabbed my hand stroking my palm with her thumb mumbling low to herself. A warm sensation spread from my palm to the tips of my fingers. I tried to pull my hand back but this fragile looking woman had quite a grip on it.

"You will soon find out who YOU really are, child, and your effect on people's lives."

My hand fell from her grip and I forgot about my change and backed away from the stand with my postcards.

Creepy old woman. My effects on people's lives? What is she talking about?

I continued to make my way through the various vendors and foods merchants until I smelled the most wonderful aroma ever. It was indescribable and made my mouth water and stomach growl at the same time. I followed the smell until I came across another old woman spooning what looked like stew into a bamboo bowl. It was a quaint little stand that was surrounded by a few mismatched table and chair sets.

I made eye contact with the woman. I studied her small frame, she wore silver everywhere. It was in her ear, on her neck, circling her wrist and fingers. Her silver bracelets made a gentle clinking noise as she seemed to float in my direction. She nodded some silent understanding that she would bring a bowl of stew.

Witch?

I shook the thought out my head. No such thing. I accepted my food and said thank you as I sat at one of the odd matched tables. The woman smiled and walked away. I held my face close to the bowl and inhaled deeply. Damn, heaven in a bowl.

I pulled out the postcards and put them on the table in front of me. I thought of the old woman at the postcard stand and studied the hand she grabbed. I could still feel her stroking my palm with her thumbs. I rubbed my hands together and tried not to think about the woman and her creepy prediction of my finding myself and the effects I have on people's lives.

I retrieved a pen from my bridal bag (which I was still carrying around until I could replace it with a decent handbag). I was about to begin filling out the postcard when the stew started calling me. I stirred it to see if I could recognize any of the ingredients. I think that's spinach, some meat (maybe goat) I thought. A tomato, some kind of peas… is that Okra? I don't like okra and although my mind instructed my hand to push away the bowl I found myself bringing a spoonful to my lips instead.

"Ummm" This taste better than it smells. I looked up to see the old woman from the postcards standing with the old stew woman. They were watching me and whispering to one another. The old postcard woman walked away but not before throwing a toothless smile my way. I knew it. I looked down at my stew only to discover it was more than half gone and even though I don't remember taking but one spoonful I had the sensation of being full. I looked up again to find the old stew woman smiling at me.

I shook off the creepy feeling I was getting and selected a postcard. Vatyra would be more worried than anyone.

I wrote:

> Life's a bitch. Then you go to Barbados.
>   Kat

That about sums that up. I looked at the other two and frowned. I thought about sending Dante an "I'm sorry" message but couldn't help wondering if I was really sorry. I wasn't sure or at the very least wasn't ready to admit it yet.

So I wrote:

> Put my shit in storage. Thanx.
>   Kat

The other card I put away. I pushed my chair away and stood. A sudden tingling sensation rushed from my ankles, up my thigh and settled between my legs in an orgasmic heat so intense my breath caught in my throat and I was forced to sit back down. I grabbed the edges of the table in front of me to steady my breathing and compose myself.

Was I panting?

This was too much. I tried to stand again when my memories of···of··· ummm, shit. What was his name? I met him at IKEA when I was picking up an office chair. His name escapes me right now but his face and body sure didn't. What a work of art.

• • •

Crayon brown skin with a chest chiseled out of marble··· Damn. The memory of him and I in his kitchen animalistically ripping each other's clothes off, slammed me back into that time and space. I suddenly felt the sensation of being lifted up and my lace wrapped ass dropped onto the cold stainless steel counter top. I felt the rush of excitement when he slid the flat side of the blade of a kitchen knife up my outer thigh, over my hip, but under my lace baby blue panties. The sudden motion of a quick tug and brief ripping sound released a growl from deep within me. IKEA man pulled the ripped pantie aside and slid his thumb over the chick in the boat and into the pulsating creamy void. I grabbed at his pants and pulled at his belt until I released a beautiful thick specimen of man meat. I couldn't even wrap my hand around it. My mouth watered. I wanted to taste him. No, I wanted to taste me on him. As if he was reading my mind he wrapped his strong arm around my waist and slid me forward on the counter. He slid into me as I came off the edge of the counter. I wrapped my legs around him, bunching my gypsy skirt around my waist. The uncut side of my panties began to slide down my thigh with each stroke. My arms wrapped around his shoulders holding on tightly for the ride. His grunts got louder, his grip tighter. I squeezed him with my pussy as I came liquid fire. I rested my chin on his shoulder and ran my hand over my forehead to wipe away the sweat and remove the hair from my eyes. My unobstructed eyes met hers and his. They were standing at the back door, just on the other side of the screen door. Car keys in her left hand, brown bag groceries cradled in her left arm, her right hand holding his left to keep him from grabbing the door handle to come into the kitchen. His right hand holding a dripping sponge bob ice pop. Our eyes stayed locked until IKEA man shuddered and began pumping furiously, slamming my ass into the edge of the counter. Her eyes dropped from mine and watched the muscles in his ass flex and release with each stroke. I couldn't hold my moan any longer or the unexpectedly fierce orgasm that ripped out of me. Her eyes, watching, it did something to me. She lifted her eyes to meet mine again, briefly, then trailed the single bead of sweat that dripped from my hair onto his back. She watched as it slowly rolled down his spine and curved over his ass until the drop stalled before dropping onto his jeans that were bunched at his ankles. He shuddered again and then plopped me back down on the cold stainless steel counter top.

"Damn girl." He said though his heavy breathing.

"Are you married?" I asked.

"Uhhh⋯" He stammered, ready to lie.

"Your wife and kid are home." I stated plainly.

"What?" He stuttered, looking at me. I tilted my chin towards the back door. He chuckled nervously and turned, settling his eyes on shocked faces. He pulled out and bent to pull up his pants. He raced to the back door and approached his wife.

"Who's that daddy?" His son asked. IKEA man ignored him.

"Honey…" He began, but she stood there shaking her head, her blue eyes filling with tears.

"Daddy told me to never trust a nigger." She spat, tossing her blond hair over her shoulder.

The word nigger froze me until I remembered it wasn't my fight. I slid off the counter and stepped out the one side of my panties. I bent to pick them up and changed my mind. I grabbed my car keys out of the sink where they were tossed in the heat of passion. I looked at the drama unfolding at the backdoor and let myself out the front.

My breaths came hard and fast as I gripped the edge of the table for dear life. I looked up and my eyes locked with the postcard woman across the table.

When had she sat down? Her eyes were cloudy and she was grinning a satisfied, smug grin.

"So it begins." She stated, laughing. "You be da cause now feel da effect." I inhaled and tried to get up and walk toward the hotel. My legs were unsteady as I willed it to move forward, away from the creepy old woman. Did this woman just put a curse on me?

My walk was slow and steady toward the hotel; my body trembled with after sex pleasures. How was that possible? How could I possibly relive something that happened so long ago in great detail? A sudden sound of shattering glass by my head had me ducking and looking around.

Nothing.

Everyone on this strip of shops were going about their business and not paying me a bit of attention. I looked on the ground around my feet and didn't see a bit of glass. But there it was again, the sound of glass crashing into something hard and then shattering to the ground. I stopped and looked around again to witness nothing out of the ordinary.

I stood still and listened.

I could hear crying and shouting and what sounded like a man pleading. I let my eyes wander over the passing crowds and could not find anything that resembled the scene that was unfolding in my head.

I tried to shake the noise out of my head and continue walking toward my room.

"I hate you!" A woman's voice screamed. *"How the hell could you fuck her in our kitchen? On*

*our countertop where I prepare food for our son?
What the fuck is wrong with you?"*

*"I'm sorry. I don't know what happened. She
walked up to me in IKEA and asked if I had a place
close by where we could fuck. That never happens
in the real world."*

*"So you give up everything to fuck a tramp in
the make believe world of our kitchen? Just
absolutely fucking brilliant!"*

"Everything?" He asked sounding panicked
*"No, not everything. We can get pass this, I love
you."*

"Fuck you!" She spat. *"I hate you. This is
done. And I'm telling my daddy what you did. You
might as well consider yourself divorced, childless,
and fired and I won't stop daddy if he decides to cut
your balls off."* She turned to walk back out the back
door then turned and said, *"By the way, I'm going to
raise my son as a white boy. He can pass as white.
Don't you think?"* She asked as she ruffled his sand
colored hair and ushered him out the back door with
promises of another sponge bob ice pop if he
behaved himself all the way to grandpa's house.

How the hell was I remembering this? I was
well away from the house while this shit took place.
I had to be imagining this. Yeah, I'm going to chalk it
up to an allergic reaction to the stew. No more

• • •

street food. I stopped at a vendor selling water and bought a bottle. I needed something to wash away my disgust. I swished the water around in my mouth and spat it out on the ground. I did this several times as I regained my strength and my stride got quicker toward my hotel room.

I ignored the sounds of sobbing and sweeping up broken glass in my head and tried hard to think of something else as I unlocked my hotel room door. I had only been here a short while and already I knew in my gut this was a horrible beginning for the new start I had hoped for.

I sat there on the edge of the bed wondering if I should just turn right around and catch a plane back home. But what would I be going home to? There isn't anyone there that would have my back. Well, maybe Vatyra, but being consoled by her comes with a price. I am not in the mood for one of her mama lectures. But for as long as I can remember If I ever needed her she was there. She was the closest thing I had to a big sister, hell even a mother. My mother was never really there for me. Her lessons always came in the form of clichés. *Use what you got to get what you want. Shake your money maker. Why buy the cow if you can get the milk for free?* Blah, Blah, Blah...

I let the thought hopping a flight back to the good ole U.S. of A play on mind a little longer while I soothed my mind with a bottle of wine and a hot shower.

Chapter Six

The days following my··· my um··· let's just call it an episode, I stayed in my room, ordered room service, laid in the sun on my deck and wrote in my journal. I had not taken the chance to even venture outside of my confined space. I gave the postcards to room service to send for mailing.

After a while I figured it was time for me to leave these walls, I wanted to see the island and do a little shopping. I needed to stop by the bank to cash in a few of my travelers cheques.

I showered and put lotion on my legs and slid on a pair of shorts and a tank top that I managed to buy from a little shop prior to running into the old postcard woman. I threw on a white wide brimmed sunhat and ventured to the great outdoors. On the way out the hotel I asked the receptionist to point me towards the bank. I wanted to be sure I went in the right direction when leaving the hotel.

The air was crisp and I took my time stepping one foot in front of the other. I could see the bank several yards in front of me, so I relaxed in knowing I wouldn't get lost looking for it. Previously I had just stumbled across it by accident. A bunch of kids rode by on a bike and their laughter filled my ears and caused a smile to creep across my face. I haven't been a fan of children for a long time, but the sound of their laughter always put a smile on my face. Their laughter was the sound of innocence before life beats the shit out of you; making you bitter and angry just for the hell of it.

Why do you have to be so self-destructive?

I remember Tamia asking me that one day during one of the rare occasions we hung out. She wanted to go out and get fruit from the Italian Market on 9th street. I took a seat on a park bench I was passing and thought about Tamia. She was in a coma back home. She was raped and left for dead in an alley. For as many things as I have done with strangers I have never felt as if I should be concerned for my safety and all she was doing was leaving work. I hated hospitals but I loved her in a sisterly way, even though we rarely saw eye to eye.

She never could understand my logic on life and I never wanted to understand hers. I felt sorry for her, raising a child all alone and obsessed with a dead man at the same time. Ok, so the dead man was the kid's father, but damn, he died over 12 years ago and I'm pretty sure she hasn't been fucked since.

I missed her though; her attitudes and all, and hoped she would come out of the coma soon.

I looked out at the water and wondered if I would ever go back to the great U.S of A.

Maybe.

Maybe not.

I was pretty much undecided.

I lingered here a moment longer before I decided I had better make my way to the bank. I wasn't sure how long they would be open. I stood and began to walk toward the bank when I heard someone call my name.

Kat? Is that you?

I turned to see who called but didn't see anything but a few people walking holding hands, some kids tossing a ball around and a woman with bright yellow shorts jogging with a golden retriever.

I continued on to the bank and only had to stand in line behind one person. I kept looking behind me out the door to see if I recognized the voice that called. I was just finishing up my transaction when I heard⋯

That is you. Oh my god. You look great. It's been such a long time.

Oh Shit. I thought. Not now in the middle of the damn bank. I quickly thanked the teller for her services and left the bank.

Hey, you look pretty damn good yourself. And, yeah it's been a while. So what have you been up too?

Hearing myself in my head was the most unnerving thing I had ever experience. I recognized his voice right away and knew what was going to happen next. I quickly contemplated rushing back to my room or settling in on the bench a few feet away. I didn't know if I really had time to do either one. I shoved my money in my purse and rushed to the bench and braced myself.

I stood there holding on to the back of that bench for what seemed like forever. I watched couples come and go and a few roller bladers roll by.

Nothing.

No voices or strange sensations.

I took a deep breath and concentrated on what was going on in my head and heard nothing, still. I decided to head back to my room and jump in the shower get a bottle of wine and lay it down.

I felt like I was losing my damn mind.

● ● ●

I quickly put one foot in front of the other in the direction on my hotel. I didn't want any unexpected "memories" to catch me lurking in the street. As I was making my way back to my room I noticed a beautiful specimen of blue black. He was···in a word··· chiseled.

Lil' Kat pulsed.

I slowed my stride and admired the sight before me. He was average height, but that didn't matter when you were lying down, bald head and naked from the waist up. The hammer hanging from the belt of his work pants made me wish he was banging me. I briefly wondered why that was the first place my mind went.

And I do mean briefly.

I watched as he tilted his head back to have a long drink out of a canister he picked up from near his feet. The pinkish liquid dropped from his full lips and hung suspended from his chin until he wiped it away with the back of his hands.

My feet moved toward him.

I had to have him.

Just once.

It's been so long; almost a full week.

I fixed my eyes on him and willed him to turn my way. I hadn't been laid since I got here, and that shit in the marketplace the other day definitely did not count.

· · ·

"Sumting I can help ya wit?" A woman's voice broke me from my thoughts. I glanced her way and lifted my chin in the direction of the blue black man. He was putting the heads of nails in his mouth. I watched my dad do that so he wouldn't have to keep reaching for a nail when he was fixing something.

"No. Thanks though. I'll be helping myself soon enough."

She didn't move. I could still feel her near me.

"Dat man already spoke fo'." She stated plainly.

"I ain't trying to marry him." I said. I could hear glass breaking in the back of my mind. A gentle reminder, I guess. "Oh well." I said casually. "Some girls have all the luck." I could barely take my eyes off of him as I turned to walk away.

I continued toward my hotel turning once to see blue black with the woman I was just talking to. She was pointing in my direction and looked to be giving him a piece of her mind. He turned and looked in my direction and our eyes locked.

Fuck that, I was going to get laid.

And soon.

"*Would you like to have lunch with me?*" The voice in my head spoke again. Shit this was going to happen now. His voice dripped sex. I knew it was in my best interest to say no. But I'm not even sure I know the full meaning of the word. Even knowing it wasn't real, not this time at least, I found myself wanting it, waiting for it, needing it. The thought of forbidden sex did something to me. It consumed me. It invited me to be...taboo.

...and your effect on people's lives.

I looked around for someplace to go as the old postcard woman's voice invaded my head. There was only the railing for the pier. I breathed deeply as I stepped one foot in front of the other toward the railing. It was only a few feet away. I reached out to grab it as everything started to change. The pier became the busy streets of Germantown Avenue in Philadelphia. People pushed as they passed by trying to get out of the street to avoid the chance of rain.

My feet hurt from those heels I just had to have even though they were a half size to small. The sky was cloudy. The weatherman had called for rain. I was mad I'd forgotten my umbrella. I was moving quickly through the street, ignoring the pain in my toes from being squished in the top of my shoes. The price of beauty is definitely pain. Then I heard it again.

His voice.

So familiar.

"Would you like to have lunch with me?" He asked again pointing to the restaurant behind us. I looked over his shoulder at the building and quickly

remembered our sex-scapade the day he married my cousin. In my defense she was a distant cousin and I was only in her wedding because she needed another bridesmaid.

He grinned at me while waiting for my answer.

"So, you want to have...ummm...lunch?" I asked suggestively.

He looked at his watch and grinned while nodding his head. I walked past him into the restaurant, but kept going until I got to the door in the back that had the stick figure of a man on it.

"For real?" He asked checking his watch again. I held the door open without responding. He entered the restroom and I followed behind him.

The men's room had balled up paper towels thrown on the floor and the floor was wet in several spots along the urinal.

He checked his watch again.

"Someplace you gotta be?" I asked as I leaned my body up against his.

"Yeah, but it will keep for a few more minutes." He said while backing me up into a stall. He pushed the lid down on the toilet and gently pushed me to sit down. My hands found their way to undoing his belt and zipper. I reached inside his pants and freed him from his cotton briefs. I licked my lips and puckered as if I was going to give his dick a kiss. I put the tip of his head against my

puckered lips and inhaled. The sensation of the cool air surrounding his tip caused him to grab a handful of my brand new lace front wig. I tilted my eyes upward to give him that lets-not-get-carried-away look, but his eyes were closed. I let my tongue guide him into my mouth. Once my lips were wrapped around his shaft I exhaled, allowing my warm breath to wrap around him.

He moaned.

I began to aggressively suck on him as he grabbed the back of my head, only letting go to quickly check the time. I released him after several minutes of oral pleasure and moved him so we could switch places.

Now he sat and I stood.

He checked the time again before lifting my pencil skirt and moving my panties to one side. He tried to bury his head between my legs while grabbing my ass to pull me forward. His tongue darted over my clitoris until my legs got weak and I had to use my hands to brace myself on the stall walls. I wanted to wrap my legs around his neck but there was just not enough room in this little stall for that, and by the way he kept checking his watching there probably wasn't enough time either.

He stopped long enough to check his watch, wipe his mouth and ask me if I had any condoms.

"You don't?" I asked.

"I'm a married man. Why would I?" He countered.

I reached in my pocketbook to break open the box of condoms Vatyra asked me to bring her for Semaj.

I tore the wrapper open with my teeth, squeezed the rubber out its wrapper, and swiftly put it on the average hard-on in front of me. I let the wrapper fall to the floor and used the back of my hand to get a short and curly off my tongue. I braced myself on his shoulders while I straddled him. I lowered myself onto him as he grabbed the sides of my thighs and rocked me back and forth. I kept trying to go up and down but he had a tight grip on my thighs.

"Let me do this." He said and I relinquished control. *"Just hold your panties to the side. I'm not trying to have this rubber break or get rug burn on my dick."*

I did as I was told.

His grip got tighter.

The rocking got more erratic.

I wrapped my arms around his back and tried to move my hips to his rhythm.

"Let me do this."

I stopped.

He leaned into me and yelled out in pleasure.

The rocking slowed. He shuddered and hooked his thumbs in the sides of my panties. He rested his forehead on my collarbone. I sat still while he slowed his breathing.

"Oh Shit" he said as he checked his watch one last time and lifted me up off his lap. He opened the stall door with one hand, pulling his pants up with the other all while using his body to push me up against the stall wall as he exited the stall. I stood looking after him with my skirt up around my waist and my pussy lips exposed because my panties were still pushed to the side. I couldn't believe he left me here in the men's room, unsatisfied, without so much of a fuck-you-very-much. I looked up to find that not only had he left me in this position but the men's room was also littered with men staring at me with their dicks in their hands. I looked toward my pocketbook hanging on the hook on the wall, briefly thought about the rubbers in my bag when common sense told me that this could quickly get out of hand. I adjusted my clothes, grabbed my bag and walked quickly out the men's room and then went across the hall to the women's room where I freshened up.

I left the restaurant to see my cousin's husband frantically pacing in front of a car with a city-boot on it and yelling into a cell phone. I started to ask if he needed help but then decided against it when I remembered how he left me in the bathroom with no regard to my personal safety or satisfaction.

I gripped the railing tight. I waited; looking around to make sure no one noticed me standing there panting and frowning. The taste of him filled my mouth and I wanted to gag. The visions or whatever the hell they were getting stronger; more intense. More...in the moment. I took a breath and looked in the direction of my hotel. I wondered if I should continue on or wait here for it. The aftermath. I knew it was right around the corner. I stood there awhile, looking out as the boats rocked back and forth in the water. It seemed like forever had passed.

I began walking when I heard a scream, a screech and then a crash. I froze and looked around slowly, hoping to see someone in distress, because that would mean I was not losing my mind. And just as before there was nothing that was going on in my head lining up with what I was seeing.

This one felt...different.

This one felt...bad. Very bad.

My heart started racing as the sound of sirens consumed the inside walls of my head.

Loud and random.

Multiple sirens.

Then the rain came. I could hear it, hitting the ground and the cars. I could hear it bouncing off the roofs of buildings. I could even smell it, mixed in with the scent of someone's freshly cut lawn. I half expected to even feel it beating down on me. I lifted my head heaven ward as an image flashed into my mind's eye.

A child.

No.

A child's limp body lying near the curb. Her clothes clinging to her from the rain. The rain washing away the red.

I shook my head. What was I seeing?

There was a group of kids on bikes clustered on one corner. They were all talking at once. They were trying to explain.

"...we didn't see her..."

"...it started raining, we were just trying to get home."

"...no, she wasn't with us. I think she was trying to cross the street."

I grabbed my head, and tried to make sense of what I was hearing, of what I seeing. What did this have to do with me?

Then it hit me. All at once, like a cosmic force out of the sky. My breath was stolen as I recalled several years ago an invitation from my cousin to a baby shower. Then the occasional family picture

Christmas card from them over the years. Then the checking of the watch as we fucked in the bathroom and finally the city-boot on the car and the frantic phone call.

"There's a problem with my car and I'm over forty minutes late in picking her up. Can you...?"

My eyes began to sting with the realization that I was looking at the blood of my blood being washed away at the curb. Her body, wet with rain, passed in front of me on a gurney. Was she...no, I refuse to even think it. I won't give that thought any energy to live. But at this point what was done was done, and wishing it away wouldn't make it so.

The doors of the ambulance closed and when they opened again I had a different point of view. It was eerily like a change of scene in a movie. I was watching that same gurney pass me again, splitting the silence with its rickety wheels on the white tiled hospital floor. The doctors seemed to pass through me as I stood there taking it all in. This could not be the result of a quickie in a public restroom. I refused to believe it.

I listened as my cousin yelled profanity at her husband as a nurse tried to calm her.

"What the fuck could you have possibly been doing that you couldn't get her from the pre-school on time? Your meeting was over hours ago. You had plenty of time!" She yelled. I watched her as she

clenched her stomach. I watched him as he shook his head back and forth while mouthing the words *"I'm sorry"* although nothing audible came out.

My head spun. I couldn't wrap my mind around it. Why would he risk it? He knew what he had to do, why would he put going to pick up his daughter on the back burner for some pussy? Even if it is *my* pussy, I smugly thought. If I'd known why he was checking his watch I would have...

I stopped mid thought.

··· your effect on people's lives.

I would have... what? Would I have stopped? Or would I have just tried to hurry up? Those questions made me uncomfortable with myself. I honestly didn't know the answer. My cousin's screaming bought me back to focusing on the scene.

"They said she was trying to walk home because it started raining." She screamed while she pounded on his chest.

He made no move to stop her.

He made no move to comfort her.

How could he? His daughter was in the operating room because of his actions. He looked up at me. My heart sank at the thought of him being able to see me.

But, he couldn't see me.

He looked through me. I turned to see what he was looking at. The police were walking toward them. He stared at them while she stopped beating on him long enough to notice a man in a white lab coat coming her way. The doctor reached them first but waited for the police to approach completely before speaking.

"The damage is extensive," he began. "she hit the base of her head on the curb causing fractured pieces of her skull to embed itself into her brain. Now, we were able to extract some but unfortunately not all of the fragments."

She fired fiery hot eye-darts at him as her lips turned up into a snarl. I wanted to leave this place. I didn't know how to. The doctor continued "at this point we aren't sure what we are going to find when she wakes. We have her in a medically induced coma until the swelling goes down. But we fully expect to see some paralysis, memory loss, and possibly some vision and hearing loss. I'm really sorry I don't have better news for you. Can you tell me how she came to hit her head on the curb?"

A policeman spoke up then but I was starting to fade. The scene was going dim and being replaced by the sights and sounds of the pier.

I tried to hold on. I needed to believe this didn't have anything to do with me.

I knew different. Didn't I?

"A woman sitting at the stop sign stated she saw the young lady get up from where she was *sitting on the steps in front of her school and began to roll towards the street on her wheelie sneakers. The woman said she saw the little girl look both ways before attempting to cross. She then honked her horn and waved the little girl across, giving her the go ahead. When out of nowhere a pack of boys on bikes sped around the corner and before anyone knew what happened the little girl was caught off balance and fell, hitting her head on the curb. The woman in the car called it in on her cell phone and made as many of the boys stay put as she could."*

I exhaled and cried as the scene faded completely away.

Chapter Seven

I paced the floor while the phone rang. I can't believe I'm doing this. I switched the phone from my right to my left ear and wiped my sweaty palms on my bare thigh. I exhaled sharply into the phone.
Ring. Ring

What would I say? I wondered and then chuckled at myself when I responded *how about hello*? The phone continued to ring and I was just about to hang up when a voice said⋯

"Hello⋯"

"Hello." I said clearing my voice.

"You have reached the residence of⋯"

"Fucking answering machine." I mumbled to myself. I tried to still my nerves. I put the receiver back to my ear so I could hear the rest of the message. I wondered if it was going to be one of those cutesy ones where he starts it and they finish it.

"Hello, is anyone there?" His voice came loud and clear through the receiver; there was a long beep as he said "Hold on the beep should stop in a sec."

He picked up the phone. My voice was caught in my throat and visions of me on that cold stainless steel table flooded my mind's eye.

"Hello. I can hear you breathing." He said a bit annoyed. "Last hello before the dial tone-"

"I've tried for years to forgive you." I managed to get out, barely above a whisper. "I still have dreams of jarred babies on poster board and wooden sticks. Sometimes they chase me through a bridal shop and sometimes through a hospital nursery."

"Maybe you should see someone about that." He said cautiously, still not sure who he was talking to.

"Like a therapist? No, thank you, I'm through trusting people with my most personal thoughts and feelings. I have a different type of therapy that works just fine for me. Well, at least it did." I spoke calmly. I had to. I wasn't sure what was brewing inside of me. Rage, Pain, Contempt, Fear, Lust. None of the above? All of the above? "You should be ashamed of yourself, professor. Married, humph, you never even gave me a choice. Heard you ended up with early retirement. No scandal for the school I suppose. You should have been jailed. More than a decade has gone by and you are still fucking up my life."

He sighed heavily into the phone.

"Katherine."

"Don't you dare speak my name." I spat

"How are you?"

"That's it? A lousy 'how are you'?"

"What would you like me to say?"

"I wanted you to say sorry, but you know what, keep your sorry. I probably wouldn't have believed it to be genuine anyway."

"Why now? I expected this call years ago."

"You have ruined my life, my vision of love, my idea of marriage and a happy home. I hate what you did to me, but, I hate that you destroyed my ideas and notions all at the same time."

"I never told you we would get married, so I shouldn't be held accountable for the destruction of your ideas of marriage. That's absurd."

"Absurd?" I gasped. "That's absurd." I mocked. "You provided piss poor example of marriage. You cheated on your wife and I'm inclined to believe I was not the first or the last···"

"You were the last," He interrupted. "My wife's step sister provides counseling to the girls at the clinic I took you too. She started there the week before; I had no idea."

"Oh, so if you would have known you would have taken me somewhere else then, huh?"

"Yes, I would have. I think that's obvious. Look, Katherine, I will take responsibility for my part in this but I will not take responsibility for your messed up vision of love, marriage or whatever else. I'm not going to be your excuse on why you can't love or won't feel or…or…or what-the-fuck-ever. I couldn't have been your only example of any life lessons, that's just not a possibility." He sated matter- of- factly.

"What?" I couldn't believe my ears.

"Fact is… you young girls never ask the right questions. I don't remember you asking if I was married and if you did I may have lied, but did you even ask?"

I tried to remember, his logic was confusing me.

"Even if you did," He continued. "and I said no, I had a very visible indentation on my ring finger and we didn't do holidays; no Christmas, New Year's or Valentine's Day. We never even celebrated my birthday on my birthday. Ever wonder why? No? Well you should have wondered. You should have paid attention. You were a smart girl; you should have figured this out. I thought you would've but…"

"So this is my fault?" I yelled into the phone. I was still pacing the floor. I could feel the sweat building up around my earlobe from pressing the phone to my head so hard.

"Well, yes. You, too, are to blame. I watched you around campus, flirting with this one and that one. You weren't looking for love, you were looking for control. When I took that from you, you didn't like it. I didn't give you a choice? A choice in what? The baby? That's a load of shit. I didn't tie you to the table and make you abort. You had the choice to leave and you did right after you added your baby to the jarred ones in your dream."

"Shut up! Shut up! Shut up!"

"Katherine, this is fact. You were not a helpless victim. You chose to ignore basic red flag issues in our situation. First,"

"Our situation? So now it was a situation and not a relationship?"

"See, again your focusing on the wrong damn thing."

"What?"

"As, I was saying, first I wore a wedding band so often I have a permanent ring around my finger; whether the band is on or not. Second, I never woke up with you in the morning. We date for over a year and there was never any foul mouthed morning breath kiss. You ever hear that expression 'don't let the sun beat your ass home'? Well, my wife meant that shit. Third, I never took any calls on my cell phone in front of you. Four, no pictures at all around my barely furnished apartment, and hardly a spare set of clothes here either. That's just to name a few. But the biggest flag should have been that I barely took you out in public."

I frowned as the memory of me getting all dressed up for a date only to be met at the door with a vhs tape and bunch of Chinese takeout buckets. We only went out in public when I would nag and even then it was about a 45 minute drive to someplace he wanted to try.

"I hate you!" I yelled

"No!" He shot back. "You hate yourself for being a whore with the best head game a man could ever⋯"

Ring.

Ring. Ring.

The sweat poured from my forehead as I sat straight up in my bed.

Ringgggg.

"Hello?" I grabbed the phone and slammed it into my ear. "Ow⋯hello?"

"This is your 6 am wake-up call."

"Thank you." I managed before attempting to hang the phone back in the cradle. "Just a damn dream." I mumbled. "So fucking real. FUCK!" I yelled to the empty bedroom. I slammed my head back into the pillow and pulled the cover up above my head. I kicked my legs up and down like a kid having a temper tantrum. I was tired of going through this. This was supposed to be my escape, gather myself together and continue to move forward. But no, I'm hearing shit, reliving orgasms with strangers and now these fucking nightmares.

The loud noise from the phone receiver being off the hook jolted me upright and cause me to slam the back of my head against the headboard.

"THIS IS SOME BULLSHIT!" I yelled laying there for what seemed like forever listening to the annoying whine from the phone. When it didn't stop right away I rolled over and pulled on the phone cord until the receiver came off the floor and was lying in my bed. I reached over to the nightstand and reset the dial tone to make a call. I paused a moment before dialing, was the dream supposed to be a message to call him? Shit was so weird right now I couldn't even be sure.

I dialed a series of numbers and held my breath.

Ring.

Ring.

Ring.

"Hello?"

What the fuck?

"Hello?" The voice asked again. "Kat, I know this has to be you. We don't know anyone else out the country. Talk to me. How are you?"

What the ···

This could not be happening. I hung up the phone and dialed another number.

"Hello?" The phone barely rang when she answered.

"What the hell is going on?" I demanded. "I just called···"

"Whoa···wait a minute now. I haven't heard from you in more than a week besides that funky postcard and this is how you start a conversation? I would hang up on your ass, but who knows the next time I might speak to your trifling ass." Her voice was calm and even but I've known her long enough to know she was annoyed and possibly even a little pissed off at me.

"Hello, Vatyra."

"Katherine." Damn she sounds like a disappointed mother. "How are you? Still in Barbados I see."

"How do you know that?"

"This is not a local number on my caller ID. Now, not that I'm not generally happy to hear from you but I know you didn't just call for shits and giggles. So what's up?'

"Why the hell did Tamia answer Dante's phone?"

"When did this happen?"

"I called there right before I called you."

"So you called me to find out what's going on over Dante's house?"

I didn't answer. The way she said it made me feel like I didn't have the right.

"Kat, what did you call Dante for? Lemme guess to torture the poor man even more? For the life of me I can't even see what he saw in you that would have him wanting to spend the rest of his life with you. I can barely stand you these days in small doses."

"That's kinda harsh, Tyra." I said frowning. I'm getting tired of everyone always jumping on me about this or that. I thought true friends were there for you whether you were right or wrong.

"Harsh? Really Kat? Lemme ask you a question. Who answered the phone when you called Dante's house?"

"I already told you." I replied cautiously. I wasn't sure where she was going with this.

"Tell me again." Vatyra's calm demeanor was starting to slip. I thought about hanging up but then I would never find out. I would just have to suck it up. I told her what she wanted to hear, that Tamia answered the phone. "So, Tamia answered, huh? Okay when was the last time you spoke to Tamia?"

Light Bulb.

I just realized where she was going with this. Shit, I hadn't even acknowledged the fact that Tamia was out of her coma. I smiled to myself then frowned when I realized maybe something was wrong with me. I mean Tamia had been in that coma for months after the rape. There were so many trips to the hospital just waiting and talking to her while she lay there in that bed seemingly lifeless. Occasionally I would think I saw a smile, but the doctors always said it was involuntary muscle movement. Shit I knew a smile when I saw one. I always wondered what she was doing in there. Vatyra spent more time at the hospital than I did but that's more her nature than mine. Should I be judged and juried because of that? Hell, I cared what happened to Tamia. I didn't care for having to take care of her slick talking son, but it goes with the duties of friendship.

"It's been a while." I finally answered.

"What fucks me up," *Oh Lawd, she done started cussin'. Here comes mama Vatyra.* She continued. "is you spoke to her and it didn't register.

● ● ●

She was in a coma for months and you've only been gone for 2 weeks at best. A lot of shit has happened since you decided to play runaway bride. A lot of people's lives have been affected."

I guess that's my fault too, huh?

"Kevin was shot by that chick you hired to help you in your boutique, he almost died that night." She paused, and then sucked her teeth. "He's fine now, thanks for asking. The physical therapy is kinda tough on him but he's handling it. He may even be able to come home soon." She said sarcastically. I didn't bother to say anything I knew she wasn't finished. "In case you were wondering, Tamia came out of her coma that same night; a news broadcast about Semaj killing her rapist jolted her back to this life."

Another pause.

"Kat? Are you even listening?" She yelled into the phone.

"Yes. I heard you."

"But. Are. You. Listening?" She pronounced each word as if I was in remedial English.

"Yes. I am. And I always told you I felt that boy was a bad seed, I could tell by…"

"Shut up!" Her tone completely threw me off. "I'm about to tell you something, that may make or break our friendship. But if I don't speak up I can't do this with you anymore."

"Stop being so dramatic…" I started before she told me to shut up again. I let her continue.

"You are so selfish and self-centered. So what, Tamia answered Dante's phone. You threw him away, remember. You have no claims to him or any ties to him at all. You sent him a postcard telling him to… to… how did you put it? Oh yeah. 'Put your shit in storage.' Do you know that a simple fucking postcard, broke his heart just a little more? No apology, no type of regret, or anything to soothe the man at all. Just plain fucking selfish. And what gets me is you weren't always this way. I know why you claim to be this way, but Fuck David. That was eons ago, get over it, be accountable for your actions. Damn, other people have problems worse than yours, and you don't see them going around breaking up marriages and sleeping with every Tom, Dick or Jane." She stopped talking. I knew her well enough to know she had stopped to choose her words carefully. "You need help. Seek some kind of mental help. And as far as Tamia and Dante go, they have both been through enough. So if they want to indulge in a little fuck-me-therapy I, for one, am all for it. Let them both move on, and if they choose to move on together, ok. And if they are just comforting each other for the moment then that's okay too. But you had your turn and you blew it. And don't you dare say anything about a girlfriend code, because I don't want to hear it. You haven't followed any codes for a very long time."

"Tyra…" I quietly started. I was really done hearing how much of a fuck up I was. She interrupted.

"Nothing left worth saying, Kat. Seek help."

Dial tone.

I hung the phone up. She was right, nothing left to say.

Chapter Eight

I sat staring at the phone awhile before deciding to jump in the shower. I poured a glass of wine and took a sip from the bottle before capping it and putting it back on the mini bar. I carried the glass into the bathroom and turned on the shower.

I sat on the toilet seat and sipped the wine while waiting for the shower to steam up.

Fuck Vatyra, Dante', Tamia' and David.

Who needs them?

I pulled my t-shirt over my head and slid my panties off. I reached for the glass of wine and noticed the glass was empty. I walked through the bathroom over to the mini bar. There wasn't any more wine in the bottle that I opened earlier so I popped open a new bottle. It wasn't chilled and for a brief moment I considered taking the time to chill it but then I decided against it as I put the bottle to my lips and sucked don't the last bit of self-confidence I had. I didn't need to be validated by them.

Fuck'em. I thought as I made my way back to the bathroom.

I poured a bit of the wine into the glass sitting on the sink. I slid back the glass door and stepped into the shower. I stood with my back against the shower wall and let the water beat down on my breast. I closed my eyes and exhaled as I wished I had a man of my own.

But I just had that⋯ didn't I?

I slid the glass door back open and reached for the glass of wine on the sink, but grabbed the bottle instead. I decided to drink myself sick tonight.

"I'm the only one that gives a damn about me." I said to the empty bathroom. "Shit, what I need is a good nut."

I giggled to myself and decided that is exactly what I was going to do. Get me a nut. I stepped out of the shower and decided to look for something I could love me with. At home this wouldn't even be an issue; I had a closet full of toys and sex gadgets. I stood at the sink and looked at my reflection in the mirror.

I pinched my nipples and smiled at the spark that ran through my body. My eyes settled on it and I wondered...just for a moment if this would do the trick. I could replace it in the morning.

What the hell. I thought as I grabbed it off the sink and stepped back into the shower and pulled the glass door closed.

• • •

I turned it on. The vibration from it made me wonder why I hadn't thought about this before. The water pelted down on my bare skin causing my nipples to become diamonds. I slid my hand down between my legs and let my fingers create their own path in the wetness.

I wanted more wine, but I wanted this orgasm more. I turned my back to the water and tilted my head under the shower head and let the water massage my scalp.

I moaned.

My hand vibrated, reminding me of my new pleasure tool. I used my left hand to spread my lips to reveal a throbbing swollen clitoris. I lowered my vibrating hand and touched my new toy to my clitoris. My breath became a distant memory as I forgot to breathe. The pleasure that ripped through me was simply...perfect. I moved my hand and moved to the corner of the shower where I could put my back against the wall and lift one leg up onto the side of the tub. I inhaled and exhaled in preparation of the intense pleasure I was about to treat myself to. The thought of it made me lightheaded as I closed my eyes and spread my lips again before letting the vibration consume me sexually.

My teeth gritted.

My leg tensed.

My breath stopped.

My toes pointed.

I screamed.

I realized at once this was a weapon; a weapon of sexual destruction. I wanted my breath back. I reasoned with my body that it was in its best interest to exhale.

My body listened. My hair stuck to the side of my face. My girlie parts tingled. And my vision blurred.

The sound of it hitting the bottom of the tub brought me back to reality.

I stared at it doing a dance at my feet as it vibrated against the floor of the tub. It caused waves in the water that moved toward the drain.

I picked it up and turned it off. I slid the glass door back and tossed it into the trashcan.

I had never felt a sensation quite that powerful; I had never had an orgasm so intense. I tried to finish showering but every touch to my now sensitive skin was like a thousand mini orgasms. I stepped out the shower. I grabbed a towel and began drying off, all the while ignoring the call from the trashcan.

I dropped the towel on the floor and reached into the trashcan when I could ignore the call no longer and pulled it back out. I went to the sink and rinsed it off. I grabbed a hand towel off the rack and dried it off on the way to the bed. I sat on the edge of the bed and pulled open the nightstand. I tossed my electric toothbrush into the drawer and made a mental note to get another one in a different color in the morning.

• • •

Chapter Nine

I was laid out on the beach, taking in how beautiful the water was. I figured I would keep the day simple, just me and a beach towel. I adjusted my bikini top, making sure everything was covered then flipped over onto my stomach I love the way the sun beat down on my back and the back of my thighs. It reminded me of a warm caress

I exhaled, closed my eyes and folded my arms under my head.

I slept.

Not long, maybe a few minutes or so before I was woken by the sound of a ringing phone. I kept my head down, resting on my folded arms, but open my eyes.

The phone rang again.

I made no moves to see where it was coming from. I already knew. It was a ring tone I had chosen specifically for Tracy's calls. I smiled at the thought of Dante's former secretary. She was a sexy one that I had an affair with; that is until she decided to go back to her hometown. Only woman I had ever been with. My smile faded when the phone rang again.

I closed my eyes. I just remembered I left my cell phone on the desk in my hotel room. Nobody was going to call me so why carry it? I was currently public enemy number one. I turned back over onto my back and closed my arms behind my head.

The ringing continued. I knew what this was, so I waited. After a few minutes the ringing just stopped.

My stomach growled.

I sat up and checked my watch; it had been a few hours since I last ate. I ignored my belly and stared out at the water.

"Tracey" I whispered her name to myself. I wondered why I was about to have one of those "flash memories" of her. All the other ones have been because my actions had caused them some type of severe repercussions. I racked my brain and cannot think of one thing that I could have done that caused her some harm. But then I again I guess I wouldn't know. Would I?

We had a mutually agreed-upon relationship. I saw her once a month and she did what she do to make me feel how I felt. The thought of it made me smile.

No... I was convinced I bought her no pain and no harm.

This time I welcome the assault on my senses for Tracy's flash memory. It had to be a good one; up until she left we were on good terms. Real good. She even attempted to initiate a threesome between Dante and I. But I had other things on my mind with Tamia being laid up in the hospital and I don't think I was ready for Dante to know what type of freak I was.

I inhaled deeply and closed my eyes. Where are you Tracy? I squeezed my eyes tight and tried to force a memory of her.

Nothing.

I stood up, shook out my towel and began walking toward my hotel. The beats of Rob Base *It Takes Two* blast in my head. I dropped my towel and dropped to my knees grabbing the sides of my head in an attempt to stop my eardrums from exploding.

A small child chased a runaway ball into the water, leaving little footprints in the sand. She was clearly laughing with glee, but I couldn't hear.

"It takes two to make things go right."

Tracy sang loud and off key in my face. She smelled like a brewery. My wrists hurt from the handcuffs. The moment I walked into the apartment she begins suggestively dangling handcuffs in front of me. She usually uses the furry ones but these look like the police issued ones. I held my arms in front of me in the arrest-me-officer position. Tracy aggressively grabbed my left wrist and slapped the cuffs on. She led me around by the empty cuff until we've reached a heating pole off in the corner of the room. It wasn't cold out so the heat wasn't on. She continued to sing off key as she looped the chain between the cuffs behind the pole and put my other wrist in the free cuff.

She was drunk and in control. I wasn't sure how to feel about that. I looked around her apartment and saw her Genie in a bottle décor was in total disarray. Jewel toned fabric and pillows were strewn across the room. An incense holder was toppled on its side but the incense in it still burned and sent a plume of jasmine and honey scented smoke into the air.

"I wanna rock right now..." I cringed at the smell of her, I hate beer. I hated everything about it, the taste, smell and the way it lowered people's self-respect. People became assholes, cried, and some became abusers.

"Can you turn that down?" I yelled over the music to be heard. She glared at me and then walked over to the stereo and cranked it up.

"Okay what's eating you?" I asked looking at her, studying her really. She had her hair twisted into a sloppy bun. Strains of it fell from the top and sides. She had on a T-shirt knotted on the side and a pair of sweatpants that hung low on her waist. I

can see the top of the Tigger tattoo she had at her panty line.

She ignored my question, but positioned herself directly behind me. I craned my neck to try and see her but I couldn't. She wrapped her arms around my waist and leaned her breasts against my back. She kissed me on my neck.

"It takes two..." She sang softly in my ear. Her hands roamed across the waistband of my jeans. She unsnapped the snap.

She stopped.

I waited.

She unzipped my jeans and folded my waistband down until my jeans were bunched at my ankles. She stood back and looked at me. The volume of the music decreased and I tried to look over my shoulder but could barely make her out. I heard moving around but she remained out of my line of vision.

"You sure are a strange one Kat." she remarked.

"How so?" I asked.

"Look at you. Expensive high heeled calf boots, nice jeans, clean white men's T-shirt and Dora the explorer panties." she tapped me on my ass.

"You don't like Dora?"

"I like her now." Tracy pulled me by my waist until I had no choice but to take a step back. As I stepped back the chain between the cuffs slid down the pole. Tracy put one hand on my back and one on

my waist. She pushed my back down while pulling my waist out. My hands wrapped around the pole to steady myself. I couldn't spread my legs to balance, because my jeans were bunched at my ankle and I couldn't take them off because I still had on my boots.

Tracy ran her hands up the back of my thighs and under the leg bands in my panties. A wave of pleasure ran through me. I was awkwardly bent and unsure of her mood. I felt her fingers spread across my ass, her thumbs over the curve of my ass and grazed over the wetness from front to back.

Lil'Kat pulsed.

I moaned.

"You like that?" She asked.

I didn't reply.

Her thumbs found their way inside.

One then the other.

One then the other.

Back and forth.

In and out.

I damn near bit my tongue trying not to scream from the orgasm that exploded from me. She just laughed as I tried to wiggle myself free.

"Where do you think you're going?" she asked through a laugh.

One then the other.

In and out.

There wasn't much more of this I would be able to take. I screamed through gritted teeth when the next orgasm ripped through me. I was sweating and started to get a throbbing pain through my lower back from being awkwardly bent this way. She didn't seem to care about my discomfort; this was very different then the way our time was usually spent.

"I have a special treat for you today." Tracey whispered in my ear as she slid Dora over my hips. She grabbed my waist and the sensation of being penetrated made me gasp, partially because she was a *she* and partially because it felt so damn good. I strained my neck to try to look behind me and see what the hell she was going through. The look on her face threw me for a loop. Her pretty face was contorted into something sinister and unappealing. Our eyes met and she took her hand off my waist and grabbed a handful of my hair and forced my head to turn in a different direction. Her hand forced the top of my head against the pole as she kept thrusting into me. Her other hand released my waist and found its way on to the top of my ass as she inserted her thumb into my ass. This was definitely a different Tracy.

I briefly wondered if I should feel violated.

Hard and fast.

She was like the energizer bunny with what I could only imagine was a strap-on. I could feel drops of moisture roll down my back and realized Tracy must be working up quite a sweat.

Her pace slowed. Her grip on my hair let up. I was scared to attempt to turn to look at her again. I felt her slowly pull out. I shuddered as another orgasm ripped through me. She stalled a bit as the tip of the strap-on lay just inside the walls of my pussy. She pulled it out and walked around to where my head was leaning on the pole trying to take some of the pressure off my hip and lower back. I turned my head slightly in her direction and I could see her legs, glistening with sweat, a large silicone penis hanging down by her inner thigh wet with my juices.

I tilted my head to look in her direction. No words. Only tear streaked cheeks. What I thought was sweat on my back···could it have been her tears? But why? She grabbed a handful of my hair and pulled my head back. I gasped in surprise. Tracy then took her other hand and grabbed her penis and slapped me in my face with it.

I closed my eyes in disbelief. My lips parted to say something when I felt her penis wipe across my face slow and steady and stop at my parted lips. I opened my eyes and looked at her. She steadied her penis right at my lips. She gripped my hair tighter in her fist, causing my head to bounce forward slightly. I tightened my lips together; I could feel my nostrils flare. I was suddenly pissed the fuck off.

"*Here.*" Tracy said, unlocking one of the cuffs off my wrist after releasing my hair. The cuff clanked on the pole as it fell from my wrists. It dangled from my other wrist swinging back and forth occasionally hitting the pole. She grabbed my hand and put the key in my palm for the other cuff. I stood slowly and stretched my back and hip, trying to ignore the throbbing. I stood there with my jeans bunched at my ankle and my Dora the Explorer panties bunched on top of that. I was reluctant in pulling them up because I was sopping wet with my juices. I needed a washcloth in the worst way right now. I looked up to see where Tracy was.

"*Tracy?*" I called into the now empty room.

"*Just go Kat.*"

"*You not gonna explain what the hell that was about?*"

No answer.

"*Well Tracy can I at least get cleaned up before I go?*"

"*There some baby wipes on the table, grab them on your way out.*"

I duck walked over to the table and grabbed the baby wipe. There was one in the package. This will not do. I went into the bathroom and grabbed a handful of toilet paper (as there were no washcloths or towels visible) and wiped away as much as I could before using the single baby wipe left.

Ever have that not so fresh feeling? I asked myself while thinking about those stupid vaginal freshness commercials and fixing my clothes.

"*Tracey, I'm leaving. You want to come out here before I leave?*"

"*Bye.*" was the sarcastic remark that came through the door to the room she was hiding in. Was she crying? I put my ear against the door and tapped on it softly.

"*Tracey...*"

● ● ●

"Get out! Damn!" She yelled as something hit the other side of the door. I turned and walked out her apartment, completely perplexed.

Back on the beach my stomach hurt.

My wrist hurt. I was panting and down on all fours. My hair hung into the sand. Grains of sand clung to several strands of hair. I had no idea what that was all about. My panting turned into sobs.

"Ms. Are you alright? Do you need any help?" A woman passing by asked.

I waved her away.

"I'm fine." I managed to get out.

"Mommy, she looks sick. Why is she crying?" a little girl asked the lady.

"I'm fine." I managed again, this time I made a point of looking up at the little girl and pasting a small smile on my face. The little girl wore a pink striped bathing suit that sagged in the backside because it was wet. My smile quickly turned to a scowl; I pushed my hair back over my head and wiped away my tears. I streaked sand across my face and was glad I managed to miss getting sand in my eyes.

"You!" I yelled, struggling to get up out the sand and stagger toward the water; beyond the little girl stood the old postcard woman. She walked along the water grinning her toothless grin. "You!" I yelled again, pointing toward the water.

"Mommy, who is she yelling at?"

I looked at the little girl as her mother began guiding her up the beach, then back at the...old ...postcard... woman. Where the hell did she go? I staggered to the edge of the water and looked to my left and right and did not see that old woman anywhere. I turned my back to the water and squeezed my eyes together tightly in frustration. My eyes burned with fresh tears and my wrist burned. I looked at my wrist and saw identical red marks from the original day I spent with Tracy. My eyes fell on the drag marks in the sand I made as I staggered to the water.

Footprints.

I turned back to the water and looked at the sand. She was here. I saw her. But there were no footprints for her. I dropped to my knees and began sobbing again. This is some bullshit. I looked for the footprints again. Where the footprints should have been there was just one word written in the sand.

KARMA.

I stared at the word. Strands of sand-infused hair stuck to the side of my face. I inhaled and made my way over to the word. Bits of sand bit into my flesh at the knees, I swiped at the letters in the sand trying to erase them one at a time. But they wouldn't move. The sand I disrupted at the K was blown away by the wind just to uncover a clear crisp K written in the sand again.

"I GIVE UP!" I yelled. "What the hell do you want from me?" I questioned in a whisper.

...and your effect on their lives.

• • •

RING.

RING.

I lifted my head and just listened. A phone was ringing and I had no idea where it was coming from.

"Hello?" A woman's voice.

"Ma..."

Was that Tracey's voice? Damn. Damn. Damn. This must be the aftermath. My head already hurts. What the fuck is next? This was supposed to be a pleasant memory.

"Tracey? Honey is that you? What's wrong?" The woman's voice was panicked.

"Ma...I wanna come home." Tracey wined into the phone. My heart flipped.

"Baby, you can always come home. Calm down and tell me what's wrong." the woman spoke calmly, pronouncing each word carefully.

"Remember that woman I was seeing?"

She told her mother about me?

"Yes, Katherine, right? Is that the one?"

"Yes, ma...well..." Tracey sniffled into the phone.

"What about her, honey. Did you two have a fight?"

"Well, she is marrying my boss and..."

"She lied to you about her sexuality?" Her mother asked cautiously.

"Um... not exactly." Tracey answered softly.

"Then what...exactly, chile?"

Pause.

Was it over? No not yet I needed to know if I was the reason she went back home. I listened for several moments.

"I knew she was my boss's fiancée."

"Okay." Her mother said, annoyance seeping into her tone.

"I knew I shouldn't but she was so beautiful... she was supposed to be a...ummm drive-by"

"She was supposed to be just sex... am I understanding that?"

"Yes...but I fell for her. Hard. Ma..."

"Tracey, I don't agree with your lifestyle but you my only child and I love you. But I did not teach you to be reckless with your choices or your..."

"Ma...not now please. You can lecture me all you want when I come home. Right now I just gotta get this shit off my chest." She said sniffling.

"Shit?"

"Sorry, Ma. May I continue?"

"I'm listening." her mother said softening her tone.

"I saw her with a man coming out of motel yesterday."

A motel...aw shit.

"So you saw her and her fiancé coming..."

"He wasn't my boss."

I gasped as I listen to this private conversation.

"So she cheated on...yall. Well doesn't that beat all?" Her mother said sarcastically. *"Tracey, honey, this woman was already cheating on her*

fiancé with you, what made you think she wasn't doing the same to you?"

"I didn't care...until I fell in love with her." Tracey full out started crying into the phone.

Love?

"Okay, okay...pack your bags. Do you need money to get here?"

"No. I'm not moving a lot of stuff back...just the basics I guess."

The conversation faded in my head. I looked out at the water and realized the sun was starting to set. I dragged my weary body back to a standing position and ignored the throbbing in my wrist, back, hip and head. My stomach growled. I ignored that too. I walked back towards my hotel. I put one foot in front of the other not even caring that I walked over the taunt that was written in the sand.

On the way back to the hotel my mind couldn't get around the fact that I was the reason Dante lost one of the best assistants he ever had. Love? How? All we did was fuck ...well kinda... she serviced me and I liked it. Where did love come from? And I agree with her mom, how could Tracey think she was the only one I was messing with?

Go figure...love. I would've basted in the glory of it if it wasn't so damn sad.

I sat there, on that beach, staring at the word Karma and wondering what kind of person I really was. I stayed there until the sun went down I finally made my way back to my hotel with the intention of heading home.

Chapter Ten

I woke with thoughts of Dante and Tamia, Vatyra and even of David. Suddenly I couldn't wait to get back home. This trip was an experience I would never forget. I just had one stop to make and that was to the old postcard lady. I was prepared, if necessary, to beg her to take this...this...curse or hex or whatever the hell it was off of me. I couldn't take the chance of people thinking I'm crazy if I had one of these...ummm...episodes in Philadelphia.

I showered and dressed in a pair of white shorts with a yellow thin strapped halter top. I oiled my arms and legs and slipped my feet into a flat white sandal. I admired my new bronze color from all the sun I'd been getting and decided I had better grab a hat so I won't start to burn. On the way out the door I grabbed my purse and a pair of sunshades I managed to acquire between episodes.

• • •

I followed the path through the marketplace admiring all the happy faces, as couples strolled hand in hand and kids ran around without a care in the world. Their lives seemed so simple and mine seem like a disaster area in comparison. I looked in the direction of where the stew lady's stand was and noticed a young woman there instead dishing out bamboo bowls of stew. I continued down the path until I came to the postcard stand. I stood a few feet away and inhaled deeply. I had no idea what I would say; I just knew I had to leave there as I originally came there.

But maybe that was the point, to leave a different person. I just hoped there wasn't any question and answer portion of getting my sanity back. I never did do well on tests.

At the counter there was a young girl with beautiful locs reading a magazine. I cleared my throat to get her attention. She didn't look up.

"Yes?" She asked "How can I help you?"

"I was looking for the older woman that was here a couple of weeks ago. She sold me..."

"She isn't here." she answered still not looking up from her magazine. I watched as she licked the tip of her finger and then used that finger to turn the page.

"Oh, when will she be back?"

"Never. She's dead."

"Oh my God. I'm sorry to hear that." She had no idea how sorry I was to hear that. "When did she pass?"

"30 years ago."

"Come again? I just bought postcards from her a couple of weeks ago."

The woman at the counter looked up at me for the first time. She had the witch's eyes. She reached under the counter and handed me a photocopy of an article. I took it and studied the picture of two women posing in front of the fountain in the middle of the marketplace.

"That's the stew woman!" I exclaimed.

"Ya, she dead too."

"No, no, no...can't be. I bought stew from her the same day I bought the postcards." I was close to tears trying to make sense of all this.

"Seem ta me dere was someting dem wan you ta know." She said tapping the photo copies she handed me a few minutes earlier. "Read dis. Dat shud help."

I looked at the picture of the 2 women again and felt sick to my stomach. Dead? I thanked the woman for her time and started reading the article in *The Nation News* some thirty odd years ago.

Grisly was the scene of an early morning 5 alarm blaze in the home of sisters Rosalina and Ahleea Coggins of Bridgetown, Barbados. Rescuers from surrounding areas were called but it was beyond salvage. As the home burned to its foundation flames could be seen dancing against the night sky for miles around. The sister's bone chilling screams where only quieted as each met a fiery demise. As glass burst out of each window in the modest home. Silhouettes of the women could be seen attempting to reach for the outside and each time something pulling them back in. The sisters who were best known for their adjacent stands in the marketplace hocking their wares daily were both seen arguing earlier that day with Elizabe Warlin. Rumor has it the argument was of a domestic nature having to do with the 2 women and her husband. No one else was home during the tragic event; there for the 5 children they had between them were the only survivors. Just the sisters perished in this horrible tragedy. When Elizabeth Warling was interviewed she was quoted as saying "Karma has an' orrible whey of comin' back ta get cha when yuh least expect it."

I looked at the woman and asked "Now what?"

The young woman closed her magazine and said "Da legend is dat dhey still walk de bay in search of somehow changing de pas by changing de future uf people like dem. So dhey make ya life a livin hell by givin a dose of da truf. Dhey show ya wut ya couldn't see witcha own two eyes."

"So when is it done? When can I get back to my life?" I asked while adjusting my sun hat.

"When ya learn da lesson the teachin will stop." And with that she opened up her magazine and continued about her day.

Chapter Eleven

I was sitting on the edge of the bed thinking about everything that I been through since I'd been here in Barbados; the visions, the voices and those damn dreams. I've had about enough and was about ready to bring this trip to an end. I wondered how I could possible get the old women to remove this... this... whatever the hell this shit is, it needs to be removed. How do you get a dead woman to do what you want her to?

I made mental plans to pack my stuff, arrange a flight and get the hell out of here.

Where will you live? The thought was barely a whisper. I had already checked on flights back home; there was one leaving every few hours. I had my credit slip from cashing in Dante's ticket. I was down to my last bit of cash anyway. My passport was in the hotel safe, all I had to do was finish packing and arrange for transportation to the airport.

I stood and walked over to the walk-in closet and began filling my arms with the clothes I bought from the various shops around town. Many still had tags on them. I dropped them on the bed when there was a knock on the door.

"Who is it?" I asked pulling the clothes from their hangers and tossing the hangers onto the floor.

"Fritz"

Fritz?

"Who?" I asked and paused so I could hear clearly. The answer came back the same. I walked over to the door and looked through the peephole.

Oh shit.

I opened the door to see blue black staring at me. I wanted to jump his bones right then and there.

"How can I help you?" I asked barely able to contain my raging hormones.

"I was tuld dat dere was an American beauty in need uf a gud time." He said grinning from ear to ear.

"Really, And how did you know it was me?"

"I ask 'roun." His answer was simple enough. He continued to tell me how he saw me staring at him, but didn't see me again so he asked around for me. He told me how he loved everything about

American women and how his wife hated them because he loved them so much.

With each word he spoke he got closer and closer until he fully invaded my space.

It started with a kiss. And all lessons I thought I learned were simply...gone.

Chapter Twelve

I lay sprawled across the bottom of the bed, legs half on half off. The white linen sheet snaked around my legs covering just enough to be legal. I opened my eyes slowly as my body registered the pain from the night before. Hair pulling and rough housing always takes a toll on me the next day, this day was no different. I'm suffering from a fuck hangover. I tried licking my lips but soon found I was also suffering from a case of cotton mouth. I lay still trying to access my body.

Thighs sore.

Head pounding.

Mouth dry.

Nipples throbbing.

Ass numb and a very weird burning sensation in my hips. I opened my eyes slowly and wondered about the time. Not quite light or dark filtered in. Sunset? No. Sunrise? Maybe. I inhaled deeply and was met with a sharp pain in my ribs. I winced, but inhaled again and sat up.

Damn, I thought, I *have to pee*.

I looked across the room and sighed. The bathroom seemed so far away.

An ear piercing ring filled the quiet room. My head pounded, and my heart jumped. The noise came again.

"Hello?" I asked quietly into the phone.

"This is your head start warning." A heavily accented woman stated calmly on the other end of the receiver.

"Excuse me?" I asked, annoyed.

Dial tone. I chalked it up to a wrong number. I wished I hadn't. I hung the phone up and slowly positioned my body to put both feet on the floor. The sheet twisted tighter around my legs. I braced one hand on the edge of the bed and the other on the night stand beside me. After shifting my weight to my hands I was able to stand. My hip burned and the pounding in my head made my body sway. I took a small step toward the bathroom and the sheet fell away into a heap at my feet. My bladder shook with the threat of releasing itself right then if I didn't get to the bathroom. I squeezed my pussy muscles to try to buy some time for me to get to the toilet. It seemed each painful step was worst then the last. I finally made it to the bathroom and caught a glimpse in the mirror as I let water loose.

I looked a hot mess! There was hardened candle wax attached to my shoulder as well as streaks of burned skin across my breast where candle wax had been poured. I don't even remember that part. After wiping and flushing I reached into the shower and turned on the water. I went back to the mirror and took a long look at myself. There were small purple and black bruises on the area right below my left ear on my neck. The impressions of teeth were clearly visible in one of the bruises. A slight impression of a hand encircled the base of my neck. My nipples looked like bruises themselves and there were more burned streaks of skin between my cleavage and across my belly from hot candle wax. I had seen enough.

I tested the water in the shower and held onto the side of the wall before lifting my foot to clear the door brace. I closed the glass door and stood to one side of the shower and just let the steam open and loosen my muscles. Out of all the pain I felt the burning in my hips bothered me the most. Maybe because most of the pain I could connect to a possible sexual position or specific sex act. This burning sensation was a mystery to me. I tried to stretch it out but it intensified. I turned my back to the shower water and stepped back into it. I tilted my head into it to wet my hair. I inhaled deeply, even though it hurt, and concentrated on the water running down my body. I took my time scrubbing the previous night's activities off me.

I towel dried and walked out the bathroom naked squeezing the excess water from my hair. I looked at the clock beside the bed on the nightstand and realized I had been in the shower for more than an hour.

What's that smell?

I stopped and inhaled. Gasoline? I dismissed it as a possible open window. I walked around the cabin and sniffed. The scent grew lighter the further into the cabin I moved. I went into the kitchen and found a half empty bottle of champagne in the fridge. I got a glass out the cabinet and made a mimosa. I downed 4 aspirin out my pocket book and chased it with the mimosa.

Naked and wandering around the cabin aimlessly I decided to do some quick sunbathing out back. I grabbed the bottle of suntan lotion that I kept by the patio door and started to head out.

"Knock, knock" a voice called from outside the front door.

"Who is it?" I asked.

"Security"

"Just a minute." I stepped slowly in to the bathroom to get the robe hanging on the back of the door. Maybe there were complaints of excessive noise from the night before. "I'm coming." I yelled when I heard the tapping on the door. I opened the door and was about to ask what the problem was when a sharp pain on the side of my head rendered me speechless. I tried to shake it off but could barely see through the red film in front of my eyes.

"You take tings dat no belong ta ya? Didn't I tell ya not ta mess wit me man?" A heavy accent spoke calmly in my ear. I could barely make out the shape of a full figured woman ⋯ or two. What the hell? Where was security? How could they not have seen these lunatics come into my room? Security was just at the door. I squeezed my eyes together and wiped at the pained spot on my head.

Wet.

I tried not to panic knowing I just got out the shower. I looked at my wet hand and lost my voice looking at all the blood.

"What the fuck?" I yelled still holding my head and backing away from these women. My vision began to clear up and I noticed one woman going from one corner of the room to another corner of the room pouring something out of a large glass jar.

She smiled at me.

● ● ●

A smile that clearly said "You done fucked up now." I turned toward the patio and figured I could make a run for it and get some kind of help. My mind forgot about my body and commanded it to move. Fast. My body quickly reminded my mind that it was less than up to the task. My hip burned something awful when I tried to turn toward the patio and run. The twisting motion made me scream out in pain and drop to my knees, she wasted no time in sending me hurling backward onto the floor after what I was sure was a boot to the face.

That was gasoline that I smelled. My heart raced and my fear rose in my throat like bile. Oh my god they were gonna kill me. No, maybe they would just beat me real bad. My mind searched for a way to get out of this. I tried to ignore the pain in my body as I crawled toward the patio door. My head snapped back as she grabbed a handful of my hair.

"I shud cut cha throat." She said calmly, like this was an everyday occurrence for her. I felt something sharp and cold on my neck. The tears streamed down my face as I thought this is what my life has come to. A one night stand and then death.

Love is overrated. I thought. *This bitch is about to kill me because I slept with her husband.*

And as if reading my mind she said, "I gon end ya cause ya disrespectful."

What's that smell?

Gasoline?

No, not this time. Cologne. No, not now, not while I'm getting my ass beat like I cussed my mama. I could smell his cologne, the strong woodsy scent of it, mixed with his sweat and the scent of my juices. The pain in my body slowly faded to pleasure as I was taken back to last night. His huge hands pawed at my body mixing pain with ecstasy. No need for buttons snaps or zippers as the tearing of fabric from my body sang a forbidden melody. The heat his palms created on my ass released a guttural roar from deep within me. My panties came away from my body in one quick motion; torn from me in the heat of passion. A quick wonder as to why I buy such expensive panties to have them destroyed by lust, entered then exited my mind. I grabbed him by the back of his head and let my tongue explore the inside of his mouth. He grabbed the back of my head, gathering my hair in his fist and turned me around. My back slammed against the slab of marble that was his chest and I inhaled sharply. I have been with many men but none had a body chiseled from stone. I arched my back and let my ass search for his dick. No luck. He tugged on my hair again and licked me from my shoulder to my ear. His tongue left a trail of liquid heat. I was drunk with passion. He bit. I screamed. He released me. I turned and was disappointed to find he was still covered in clothes. He must have noticed my expression and magically the clothes were in a heap at his feet. I stared. I couldn't help it. What a specimen. He was the color of a starry night; black with shades of blue filtered in. His eyes twinkled mischievously. I studied his chest and arms and thighs. In a word? Perfection. Not a flaw on his washboard abs. I let my eyes roam over his body taking in everything. Finally I rested my eyes on what I wanted most at this moment, his thick blue black dick. *What the fuck?* You have got to be kidding me. Before me stood this beautiful specimen of man meat, with a blue black pencil dick. Where is the thick blue black dick I was sure to find? My smile slowly faded. *What a waste of a great body*. He reached for me. I stepped back, my lustful high quickly dissipating.

"No regrets." He said, obviously having had this reaction before. *"You will be satisfied."* He said stepping into my space.

Whateva.

I reached for a glass of wine I had on the table just off to the left of him and knocked it back. As I leaned to put the glass back on the table he bent and his tongue circled my nipple. He pulled me close and began to trail his tongue down my belly, past my belly button where he stopped short. I bent my head to look at him there on his knees just looking at my pussy.

Why did he stop? I wondered. I *was freshly showered.*

"Come" He said, standing. He took my hand and led me to the bed. *"Wait."* Then he walked into the bathroom and returned with a towel and a plastic basin of water, a razor and a bar of soap. I know he wasn't about to do what I think he was about to do. I wanted to fuck not play barber. He laid the towel on the bed and gestured for me to sit. I did. He knelt in front of me and put my breast in his mouth. I moaned. He slowly slid me back onto the bed. His lips caressed several spots on my body on the way to my pussy. I could feel myself getting hot and moist between my legs.

With my eyes closed I could feel his fingers running through my down-there-hair. He was soaping it up for the big shave. I didn't want to be shaved, didn't he understand that I wanted to be fucked and nothing he did down there was going to make me forget about his pencil dick. I sat up on my elbows and peeked down my body to look at what he was doing. I giggled to myself at the intense expression on his face as he slid the razor over my soapy hair. I leaned over to the nightstand and grabbed the bottle of wine.

"Steady." He said.

"Yeah, whateva, just hurry up. You are killing my buzz." I stated plainly putting the bottle to my

lips. I sipped slowly and briefly wondered how I got here. He was just so damn fine when I first saw him nailing those boards out by the bank. I ran into him again at the beach that night his baby-mama told me to get lost. Fuck her I do what I please. Like now I'm about to do who I please. I need a real lay, even if it is with pencil dick. I took another long sip when I felt him run a cool wash cloth across my now bare pussy. I looked down my belly to see a very thin landing strip where my short and curlies used to be. I sighed and moved my elbows so I was flat on my back again.

He moved slowly to the table in the middle of the room placing his shaving supplies on it. I watched him move. I watched his blue black buttock tense and release with each step.

What a fucking waste of a great body.

I closed my eyes and waited for his next move. I could feel him straddle me. His nuts warm on my belly. His fingers trailed from my belly button between my cleavage and up to my chin. I licked the tip of his finger when he touched my lip. Soapy. I ignored that and grabbed his hand and kissed the inside of his wrist.

He moaned.

I moaned too.

I mean, why not, fake it till you feel it, right?

He inched his body up mine until he was nut-to-lip level. I stuck my tongue out and he leaned his body forward, putting his balls in my mouth. He grabbed the back of my neck and pulled it up, shoving a nearby pillow under it.

After a moment or two of cradling his balls in my mouth he attempted to put his dick in my mouth. I felt like I was getting my lips together to whistle instead of stretching my jaw muscles like I'm used to. After sucking his···after sucking him briefly, he started to move himself slowly down my body kissing and licking. He stopped and admired his handy work, gently licking the landing strip. He picked up the spilt bottle of wine and began to pour what was left, which wasn't much, of the bottle on me. He licked my belly button, removing splashes of wine from it. He also licked splashes of wine off my hips and thighs before roughly parting my legs.

I moaned and thought about how much I wanted this man...that is before I saw him fully naked. What a waste, but here I was... here we were, naked and covered in wine. His tongue slid over the top of my pussy and I nearly shuddered out my skin. It was such an unexpected ripple of pleasure. Who knew the skin on top was just a sensitive, if not more, than the skin in between. I let myself relax while blue-black went to work licking and kissing the top of thighs and pelvic region. I slid my hands over my belly and dipped my ring finger into my belly button slightly. It was wet. I lightly fingered my belly button while he continued to explore south of my body. The little jolts of electricity coming from my navel and pubic area were causing my nipples to stand erect. I looked down my belly to see he was really into what he was doing. I slid my hands up to caress my breast and squeeze my nipples. I arched my back and opened my legs wider when I felt his head dip down further between my legs. He moaned as his tongue circled my clitoris sending sensual vibrations throughout of my body. His pace of his licking increased. He grabbed my hips and began to pull me into his face. He lapped at my pussy as if he hadn't eaten in days. He was hungry for me and the thought of that truly turned me on. I tried moving my hips round and round but he restricted my movements. I grabbed at his head, I needed him to slow down or I was going to...

"Oh shit..." I panted. I could feel my body begin to shake with pleasure. My breathing became erratic. I pushed at his shoulders and felt him lock his hands into my hips as his arms snaked under my knees. Not wanting him to stop but wanting him to release me at the same time I found myself wrapping my legs around his head. *"Oh, Shit!"* He released me on one side and I felt his finger slide past his tongue

over my clitoris and into my...ass. I bit down on the corner of my lip and stifled a moan. His tongue followed his finger down and began to flick in and out of my ass alternating with his finger. The rhythm he created caused me to pant and squeeze my eyes shut. I concentrated on the feeling that was leaving me orgasmic-ally paralyzed. It started at my toes and slowly rolled up my legs toward my thighs I wanted to grab him and let him fuck the shit out of me. I was scared his pencil dick would kill the mood. I managed to scoot from under him and turn to get on all fours. I reached into the nightstand and pulled out my electric toothbrush. As he entered me I reached between my legs and turned my toy on allowing the soft bristles vibrate back and forth over my clitoris. He didn't enter right away; instead I felt a burning sensation flow down my back and then another sensation flow from the top of my shoulder down to my breast. I looked at my breast just in time to see the candle wax begin to harden.

He penetrated me with something round and hard, but by the way it felt I knew it definitely was not his dick. I looked back to find he had taken a candle stick from the holder on the table and was using it to fuck me with. A part of me wanted to object, but how could I when it felt so damn good. After a while he removed the candle and inserted his own dick. I squeezed my pussy muscles and rocked my body back and forth in an effort to help him hurry up and cum. I was beginning to feel exhausted from all the orgasms. I was amazed at how his dick felt like I was being fingered instead of fucked.

Finally, he came. It must have been a hard nut, too, because he grabbed my hips and began bucking wildly. After he caught his breath, he kissed me on my forehead and made his way to the shower mumbling something about how his wife could smell an American woman on him.

I waved him away to the bathroom and wrapped the sheet around me. I don't know how long he stayed or when he left and I didn't even care.

The smell of gasoline and the heat of the blaze slowly began coming into to focus. I was lying on the ground while the woman I now recognize as the Caribbean woman that told me he was spoken for was his wife. She was here and she was beyond pissed. I tried to curl my body into the fetal position as she kicked and stomped on me. She even spit on me and called me all kinds of names, some I knew and some I didn't. The other woman she came in with was calling her name and telling her they had to leave now or else they would burn up with me.

She hesitated before giving me one last kick to the face and spitting on me. I laid there among the thickening smoke. I could feel the heat from the flames, and for a brief minute I thought maybe I should just lay here and be engulfed in them. Then I thought of the old women and their stories and how they perished by fire. I covered my mouth and nose with my hands and tried to crawl to the glass door that led to the deck. It was closer than the room door.

I made it to the door and attempted to stand. The smoke was too thick and I was in too much pain. But I could not reach the door handle from on the floor. I started coughing as my lungs began to fill with smoke. I started thinking about how I was going to get out of here. I started thinking about all the people I left behind and all the people I had hurt. Then it dawned on me...this was my aftermath. I was living...or getting ready to die in my very own aftermath.

I pushed at a brass coat rack that was beside the door. It rocked slightly. I pushed at it again mustering up a little more strength. It rocked and then finally fell through the glass door, shattering it. I crawled quickly to the door. I could hear sirens in the distance. Would they make it here in time to save me?

Save yourself. It was the old postcard woman's voice. I looked up, past the door and the glass and saw them dancing on the beach, the sisters. I could feel myself fading, but their chant for me to save myself gave me hope and little more strength. I attempted to crawl across the glass out the door onto the beach. The pain from the shards of glass and the broken bones I was sure I had were too much to bear.

I failed.

That was the last thought I had before everything went black.

Epilogue

As I sat on the beach, beaten and bruised, squishing sand between my toes I looked out at the water. My only possession was the smoke filled clothes on my back, and the passport in the hotel safe.

I'm stuck here. I'd rather be dead. I thought.

I watched as a firefighters worked to put out the blaze. I wondered how I had gotten this far down the beach. Surely I hadn't walked it, or crawled it for that matter. I could barely breathe and sitting up was a chore in itself.

Maybe I'll lie here and die from internal bleeding.

It was a welcome thought, even if it was just for a moment. The sounds of laughter and conversation caused me to look up. There was a

● ● ●

group of people strolling on the beach, talking and taking in the breeze from the water. They were talking about going down the beach to watch the firefighters.

As the crowd passed by I heard a woman say "I think I know her...Kat? Is that you? Oh my god, what happened to you?"

The nice woman who took my wedding shoes and gave me flip flops in return stood over my soot darkened body.

I wanted to speak. To confirm that, yes, it was me. I could barely nod a confirmation.

"Help me. Somebody help me get her some medical attention." She spoke rapidly to her friends. "Can you hear me? I'm going to get you some help. Dear God..." She began to pray over me as she helped me to lie down. She removed her sweater and put it under my head. "Just stay with me. Is that your hotel that's burning? Oh, lawd, why am I asking you questions when you can barely speak? Jesus be a healer, we need you now!"

Hours later I woke in a hospital room with her by my side. She was reading a magazine.

"Well, hey there. How you feeling?"

"hmmmm..." I tried to speak but it hurt.

"It's okay, don't try to speak. I did manage to get you some clothes, since you were on the beach in your robe. I also talked to the hotel and they told me you were attacked in your room. They have the woman in custody; apparently this wasn't her first time assaulting American women. Unfortunately everything you had in your room was destroyed. I'm sorry."

I turned away from her and started to cry.

"I want to go home..." I managed to say.

"Ok"

A few days after the attack I was on my way to the airport; Nicole made arrangements to get my passport from the hotel and acquire me a plane ticket. I told her I would pay her back just as soon as I got back home. She told me not to worry about it and her mother would be proud of her for helping someone in need. She gave me her phone number again and this time I stuck it in my pocket. I might have room for one more friend.

On the way to the airport I had the driver stop at the postcard stand one last time. I bought 1 postcard. On it I wrote:

Dante,
      I'm sorry.
            Kat.

The End

Between My Legs   Junnita Jackson

www.ingramcontent.com/pod-product-compliance
Lightning Source LLC
Chambersburg PA
CBHW052144170626
46812CB00004B/1576